A STORY BY
MARY HELEN BROWN

Solomon & George Publishers
108 S 8th Street
Opelika, AL 36801

1. Texas - Fiction. 2. Southern Culture. 3. Humor

ISBN: 978-0-9966839-3-7

First Edition

Cover design by Iris Saya Miller

Any resemblance to real people or places is either intentional or coincidental. If you believe you recognize yourself, someone or some place and you like it, then the resemblance is intentional. If you believe you recognize yourself, someone or some place and you do not like it, then the resemblance is entirely coincidental.

"You can always make a good story better."

—Edward Eugene Bishop

Tommy Austin

Tommy Austin getting killed by the angel was the first strange thing to happen that summer, but it certainly wasn't the last.

Since it was first, though, I probably ought to tell you about it. You see, we played baseball in the cemetery. We weren't supposed to, I guess, but we did anyway. The town leaders had just bought this whole new property and were going to expand the graveyard as more of its citizens went on to their greater reward. But for now it was just a big old empty lot without any pine trees, just aching for a ball game. The monuments and graves and stuff didn't really get in the way. I always liked to pretend that I was out in Yankee Stadium and those monuments said Ruth and Gehrig and DiMaggio—not that I'd ever seen Yankee Stadium other than watching it on TV. Shoot, if I could get my imagination really going I could just about see my name out there on my very own Yankee Stadium monument.

Then I'd come back to myself and there I'd stand in right field next to the Walker family—Paul, Janice, June, and Eunice—God holds them in his bosom. I played right field a lot—right field being where you put the person who is a year younger and two years less coordinated than anyone else on the team. Every so often, when a southpaw would come up, I'd trot over to left field and visit with the Allens, but most of the time it was me and the Walkers.

Tommy Austin was the center fielder and probably our best player. No, I take that back, Jodell—we called her Smitty—was our best player. She was our shortstop and could throw like a cannon. It didn't matter if you were a boy or a girl on this team if you could play, and Smitty could play. Anyway, Tommy Austin was the best boy on the team, and he played center field. He played out there instead of pitcher or something because he thought he was the next coming of Willie Mays.

Tommy's closest companion in center field was Miss Purcell. Miss Purcell (capital Miss) was a legend in Rowja. My granddaddy called her "that pinch-faced old-lady school teacher." The woman was long dead by the time I came along, but she had taught English and declaiming in the schools for sixty years. She taught my granddaddy and my daddy and when they got in the mood they could talk about Miss Purcell all through Sunday dinner. I never met her, mind you, but apparently she was the palest woman ever to set foot on the earth, had hair a color God and Clairol never even thought of, owned three cotton dresses of the same pattern but different colors, and was mean. According to my daddy, Shakespeare didn't have to write as many essays as they did.

But like I was saying, Tommy Austin was out there with Miss Purcell. She kind of stood off from everybody else, and all the guys at school said it was haunted. She had this big old monument on her grave. It was an angel with his finger pointing to heaven. My granddaddy said it was because Miss Purcell needed the directions. If you walked past her grave when the moon was full and said "ain't," that angel was supposed to lower that finger and point it at you. I never tried that.

That day, the sun was out, and it wasn't even particularly hot—90 or so. There weren't any funerals, so we could have a game. It was about the fifth inning when it happened. Our team was ahead by the disputed score of 13 to 9. Our players thought we had 14 runs; their team thought we had 12. Their power hitter, J.T., was coming to bat, so everybody backed up a little. You didn't want anything to get past you because it would go bouncing around amongst those tombstones. So Tommy Austin was standing pretty close to Miss Purcell when J.T. gave that ball a ride. Tommy turned around to make one of those over-the-shoulder Willie Mays catches and ran slap into Miss Purcell's angel.

Now I don't know why it happened—maybe it was all those guys who'd gone up and pushed on the angel trying to wake Miss Purcell up, maybe it was all those baseballs that had banged into the angel, maybe Miss Purcell was just still mean—but that angel came a-loose, fell over, and squashed Tommy Austin flat. The spooky part was that now that angel's finger was pointing at me and the Walkers.

Like I said though, that was just the beginning. The weekend was when things really started coming together. They held Tommy Austin's funeral, tried to fix Miss Purcell's angel, and my sister came home to announce her summer project.

Tommy Austin's funeral was a sight. Since Tommy was so young, he drew a bigger crowd than usual. Now I'm not being ugly about this or anything, just realistic. In Rowja, funerals were social occasions and the weirder the way you died, the younger you were, and the more prominent you were in the town, the more likely you were to draw a crowd. Since Tommy Austin's daddy was the high sheriff of the county, his funeral had all the makings of a whopper.

The funeral was at the First Baptist Church there on Church Street. Church Street was named right. They were lined up there like a shooting gallery—First Methodist, First Baptist, First Episcopalian, First Presbyterian, First Assembly of God—I don't know if they actually all started with First, but it seemed like they did. Anyway, all the main branch churches were right there together except for the Church of Christ, but then they *would* be separate. So where most towns have a fast food row, we had church row.

The coffin was closed—for which I was eternally grateful, but for which some other folks had seemed disappointed. Those other folks hadn't seen Tommy Austin right after they'd rolled that angel off of him. I had.

During Tommy Austin's funeral the preacher talked, a brass quartet from the high school band sputtered though "Rescue the Perishing" and several folks had hay fever attacks from all the flowers. It was then that Bertie tuned up.

Bertie wasn't dangerous; she just had some peculiarities. Like I remember that time it came across on the news that one of those satellites might come out of orbit and crash. Well, Bertie took to wearing a motorcycle helmet around town for protection. Granddaddy said nobody had anything to worry about as long as they stayed away from trailer parks, but Bertie wore that helmet for weeks anyway.

Bertie's great talent was that she could fix zippers. She would say that she could fix the zippers on pants and that you didn't even have to take them off. Nobody in my family was the least bit interested in seeing if she could, but if a sample salesman ever came in the store while Bertie was there, my granddaddy would ease over to her and say, "Bertie, that fellow over there sure does need help with his zipper." Then he'd watch the poor fellow run all over town with Bertie in hot pursuit hollering, "I can fix your zipper!"

Bertie also carried around all her personal belongings down the front of her dress. My sister—I'll tell you more about her later—told me once that Bertie looked like she belonged on the front of a ship, but was probably flat as a fritter underneath. All I know is that you never really knew what size or shape Bertie was going to be.

Bertie's big concern was germs. She'd wear gloves all the time and sometimes she'd have a red or blue bandana covering her nose and mouth. No matter how hot it was, she'd wear this long old red coat with a mangy fox collar. She was a walking cough drop dispenser. To her, coughs were the present day version of the rats that carried the plague fleas around. So if she'd ever hear anybody cough, she'd cover her face with her bandanna, scurry over toward the carrier, and chunk a red Luden's cough drop in his general direction. My sister and her friends used to scatter out in church and take turns coughing, and they'd have Bertie scrambling all over that building. One time when they were relay coughing my granddaddy let out a little "auhgugh" and then turned and winked at me. None of the other grown-ups seemed to know what was up, but then again I'm not so sure my granddaddy ever really did grow up.

At Tommy Austin's funeral, Bertie got going big time. Right after the preacher finished reading the 23rd Psalm, Bertie started moaning. We all thought she was going to start speaking in tongues again. But no. She just sat back there and made this moaning noise. So folks thought she was grief-stricken. Why, I don't know. She wouldn't have known Tommy Austin from Willie Mays. Later on, though, about the time the choir was letting fly with "Rock of Ages," Bertie started shouting clear as a bell, "The sins of the fathers are visited upon the children . . . The sins of the fathers are visited upon the children . . . The sins of the fathers are visited upon the children . . ." That went on for the entire first verse. I guess everybody thought she'd settle down after a while but she switched to chanting, "Repent, repent . . . the past becomes future . . . Angels fall from the skies . . . Repent, repent . . . The past becomes future . . . Beware . . . Angels fall from the skies . . . Beware . . ." Now mind you, an angel had fallen, but it didn't fall that far and at the time I thought it had to do more with Tommy Austin smacking it a lick than any sign from God. I don't know how long Bertie kept it up; she'd seem to get tired of one message and switch to another. They all sounded pretty much the same. Miss Purcell's angel falling was some sort of sign that bad times were coming. Now like I said, Bertie's chanting kept up for a good spell and after a while folks started giving out these little nervous laughs and coughs and stuff. I guess Bertie's cough phobia was stronger than her religious inspiration because presently she stopped shouting and took to chunking cough drops around.

They finally got the service over with and everybody loaded into their cars, pulled on their lights and headed for the cemetery. A police escort led us wrong way around the square. It didn't cause much problem even though it was a Friday because most of the stores were closed for a couple of hours out of respect for Tommy Austin's family. About the only ones that were open were the big discount stores out on the loop.

The square is right in the middle of the town, but despite its name, people say they drive around it. It was a one-way, two-and-a-half lane, all rules barred squared-off race track around the courthouse and city and county offices. Most of the home owned businesses, the picture show, the banks, and the post office were on the square so there was usually a pretty good portion of traffic. Now, like I said, this was no-rules driving—the lanes weren't marked, and there didn't seem to be any speed limits. To figure out if somebody was changing lanes or was going to turn or something you didn't look for a blinker, you tried to look them in the eye.

I've seen folks from out of town get stuck in the inside lane and have to go around five or six times before they could get off on one of the side streets. Local folks usually only had to go around twice at most, because one of the first things you learned when you learned how to drive in Rowja was how to bull your way on and off the square.

There weren't any laws about the size or kind of things coming around the square, so you had to contend with big old chicken trucks and pulpwood trucks that couldn't quite make the turns. And you had to watch out for the folks parked on the sides. You could park slant-wise on either side of the traffic lanes, so folks were always backing out right into traffic. When my mom taught all of us how to drive she had us going right down the middle in the half-lane because there was more room to dodge. You can ask anybody who has ever driven through East Texas if they've been on the Rowja square, and they'll tell you the same story. I'm not lying.

It didn't take long to get out to the graveyard. In Rowja, it doesn't take long to get anywhere. I was pleased to see that they were burying Tommy Austin in the old part of the cemetery with the rest of the Austins. It would have been bad if we'd had to step on Tommy Austin on our way to third base or something. Miss Purcell's angel was still laying out there in center field, pointing toward the Walkers. All in all, the graveside service went real smooth, probably because Bertie hadn't been able to get a ride with anyone. When she'd get close to a car, somebody would cough, and she'd sling a Luden's through the window and move on. Out-of-towners probably thought we were having a whooping cough epidemic.

A couple of guys talked about getting a game together later on that day, but somehow it just didn't seem right to be playing ball there with Tommy Austin laying out there fresh dead and all. Besides, we didn't have a center fielder until my sister came home. She could cover until we found a new one.

It was Saturday morning before a few of us went out to the cemetery to practice throwing and batting the ball around. Most of us had packed sack lunches and Lester Finch, whose daddy ran the bottling plant, had brought a big cooler full of Co-Colas, so we were planning on making a day of it. We didn't get to have much of any kind of practice though, because of Miss

Purcell's angel. It wasn't that he was in the way or anything; it was that the cemetery committee and some other volunteers from the First Baptist Church had decided that Miss Purcell's angel ought to be set back on his perch before it rained or something. We offered to help, but they didn't seem interested. So we all settled down next to some tombstones and watched the proceedings. Now, I'm not going to name names or anything, because there were words spoken that good Baptists shouldn't have been saying. My granddaddy and, in fact, my entire family would say them, but none of us ever claimed to be *good* Baptists. The men working on Miss Purcell's angel professed to be good Baptists though, and they were letting fly with some especially nice ones. My granddaddy always said there were two kinds of cussing. Cussing you could find in the Bible and serious cussing. This was serious cussing.

Apparently, Miss Purcell's angel was heavy and bulky and that arm with the pointing finger kept knocking people in the head. Jodell allowed as to how it would be bad if Miss Purcell's angel killed Tommy Austin and then poked somebody's eye out. We all thought that was pretty funny, but those men shot us a look when we laughed. Come to think of it, Miss Purcell would have been proud of the look they gave us.

What they were doing was, half of the cemetery committee would get on one side of the grave and pull on some ropes and the other half would push on the other side. Either the pullers were pulling too hard or the pushers were pushing too hard, because they never could get Miss Purcell's angel balanced long enough to get it set. They'd get Miss Purcell's angel on top of the monument, then it'd start to tilt and the cemetery committee would start yelling to watch out, then Miss Purcell's angel would tump over in the opposite direction and the cemetery committee would commence to cussing.

Finally, a couple of them figured out that if they'd go get some sort of block and tackle things might go a bit better. So they went off to borrow one. After a while they backed a tow truck up to Miss Purcell's grave and tried to get her angel harnessed up. I have to give them credit; they ran the thing pretty well considering the number of people giving directions. They swung Miss Purcell's angel around a while and finally got it to sit pretty still up there on its place. It just tilted a mite. They worked on it a while, got it stable, congratulated each other, disconnected the truck, and left. Trouble was, Miss Purcell's angel wasn't exactly pointing toward heaven anymore; it seemed to be pointing more toward Shreveport.

While we were out at the cemetery, I saw my sister go by in her car. My sister's car was unusual for Rowja. For one it was a foreign car—a VW Beetle—one of the few foreign cars in Rowja. Lots of people in town expressed the opinion that if we fought the Germans in World War II, we shouldn't be driving their cars. My sister allowed as to how we fought the Mexicans for independence, and we were still eating tacos. I never knew what one had to do with the other, but her reasoning seemed to work. The other reason my sister's car was unusual was that it was blue. Not sophisticated navy blue or soothing blue, but bright blue like you might see on a neon sign for a seafood restaurant. So when my sister drove by, there wasn't any question who it was. I struck out for home.

I probably ought to introduce you to my sister a little better before I tell you about the surprise. My sister's name is Melanie Catherine, a name that came out of a fight. When my sister was born, everybody had their own personal favorite name—favorite aunts' names, grandmothers' names, mother's name, and on and on. My mother got fed up with the whole thing and, being a *Gone with the Wind* fan, told the doctor the baby's name was Melanie. Since there was an Aunt Catherine on both sides of the family, each side thought she'd been named after that Catherine. Actually she was named after Catherine Street where my mother had grown up in Shreveport. My sister never liked her name that much, but allowed as to how it could have been worse—Scarlet Main or Prissy Elm.

Getting Home

Of course, my sister beat me to the house, but I wasn't far behind. She was on the porch being greeted by Buddy and Lady, the mostly collies, and Zeus, the house cat/puma mix. It was an accepted rule that girl dogs were named Lady and boy dogs were named Buddy and that we didn't have cats. Those rules had been in place at least since Daddy was a little boy, but they were aimed at our official pets. Over the years, we'd had any number of pets that had just come up, and they were not subject to the naming rule.

The cat Zeus, a two-rule violator, was one of those. Zeus was special because our mother had announced that "two dogs were plenty and we don't keep cats" when she found that Sister had snuck him onto the screened porch. At that point, he was just a kitten and had not grown to his full massiveness. Sister kept bringing him in however. One day, about the time Mama was going to go into a full-fledged get that damncat (her name for Zeus) outta here speech, Zeus came walking up carrying a mouse that had been troubling Mama for months. Mama was so smitten with "such a good boy" that she went and boiled up some shrimp for "the best fellow ever." She then proceeded to lecture the rest of us on how Zeus was the only one who ever helped her keep the house nice.

I never really understood Mama's two-pet pronouncement anyways. We always had more than two animals. We lived just a little ways from one of the local vets, and people were always dumping animals thinking she'd take care of them. She wouldn't, but my daddy or grandmother would. So we had a rotating cast of dogs and cats and even a guinea pig or two. Shoot, even Zeus' mama cat was an intermittent resident. Her name is Rowrr, pronounced, "rowrr." She got her name when my grandmother said, "Well, I haven't seen you around here before. What's your name?" Clear as a bell, the cat said rowrr, so Rowrr it was. Rowrr is as wild a cat as you'd ever hope to meet. She'd vanish for months at a time until she'd wander up, pregnant. She'd start off at the vet's barn where she'd deliver a litter of kittens. We figured she wanted to be near the vet in case there were problems. Nobody was allowed near her or the kittens until Rowrr decided the time was right. Then, she'd pick them up one by one, trot them down the road to our place, and put them in the carport. She knew my daddy would take over their care and likely as not find them a good home. She would also allow us to feed, but not touch, her for a while. Zeus stayed because he took to following my sister or me around like a dog, and I suppose that made him acceptable. Buddy and Lady even tolerated him.

Anyhow, the pets were all excited that Sister was home, and my arrival increased the celebration.

"'Bout time somebody came home," she said. "If it weren't for the dogs, I'd have my feelings hurt." She knew that it was likely nobody would be home. Mama and Daddy were at the store.

"Hasn't the phone rung yet?"

"Nope, and I've even been to the bathroom."

Usually the phone rang almost immediately upon anyone's arrival. Mama swore that our grandmother, Daddy's mama, kept our house under surveillance. She'd see somebody come home and then time her call to match the approximate time it took for any of us to get in the house and sit on the pot.

"Never mind, I forgot. She was going to get her hair done today."

"God help the ozone layer. Is there anything around here for dinner?"

"There's some leftovers from supper, some slices of works from the Pizzazz, baloney for sandwiches, some ever-loving soup, and just general stuff in the cabinets."

Works pizza had everything on it that the Pizzazz used on a pizza except for anchovies. We don't eat anchovies. Ever-loving soup was always in the icebox. It was a soup that Mama just added to. She used whatever happened to be leftover that might taste good in a soup. Every so often she'd pour a couple of cans of diced tomatoes in the pot just to keep it soupy. You never quite knew what you'd get in ever-loving soup, but it was mostly good and even if it wasn't all that great that day, a little Tabasco would fix it right up.

"I'd just as soon go eat at the store. I need to talk to Mom and Dad about something and maybe they won't be too busy. That suit you?"

"Suits me fine." It really suited me more than fine, but I didn't want to let on.

"Let's go ahead and go before Me-Mama gets home from the beauty shop. I don't want to have to account for everything I have or haven't done since the last time I was home."

"You'll do that soon enough, I imagine."

We made our apologies to the pets, piled into the car and headed to McRiley's Medicine and Mercantile.

McRiley's was the family business and had been for years, though not a one of us was a McRiley. Mr. McRiley had founded the store way back yonder in Mayhaw, where my granddaddy had grown up. Granddaddy had gone to work for McRiley's Mercantile after he'd quit school. He quit school when he jumped out a window to avoid taking a Latin test.

Granddaddy's daddy told him that if he didn't go to school and was too lazy to work on the farm, then he might as well get a job in town. So he went to work sweeping and straightening at McRiley's. At this point, things get a little cloudy what with Granddaddy telling the story and all.

McRiley's carried just about everything a store could carry, including some patent medicines. Apparently Granddaddy had always been good at tending to the sick, and animals, and even other kids. So over time, Granddaddy took to being in charge of the medicine section and working with the local doctors. He also became good friends with the local druggist, an older gentleman, and started learning about that trade. He got to the place where he started mixing up his own medicines, a couple of which got to be well-known in the area: Cotton Pickers Lotion and Cry Baby Medicine. About this same time, he picked up the name Doc. It suited him better than his real name, Sylvester Ferrin.

That part of the business was doing so well that Mr. McRiley hired the druggist and bought out his stock. He then changed the name of the store to McRiley's Medicine and Mercantile. After a few years, the druggist retired, and Granddaddy became the local druggist. The rules for dispensing prescriptions were looser then. The McRileys didn't have any children, so they left the store to Doc, and that's how we came to own McRiley's even though we aren't McRileys ourselves.

Doc ran the store himself for a fairly long time and came to be known for his commonsense approach to medicine. He also knew a whole lot about drugs and how they'd act and interact. Real doctors would call him up on a right regular basis to make sure that their patients weren't going to other doctors trying to get too much medicine or to find out if the medicines they were prescribing were going to mix together all right. One of Granddaddy's favorite things to ask young doctors was and still is: "If you are going to give a fellow a sulfa tablet every 3 hours, how many tablets will you give him in 24 hours?" He'd wait for them to say, "8" and then point out the correct answer, which is 9.

After World War II, the population of Mayhaw began to fall off, so Doc decided to move the business to the booming metropolis of Rowja. One of the local pharmacists had died and the city council was looking for a store to fill the gap. About this same time, the state pharmacy board was beginning to butt into the business as well. It seems like they were none too happy about a prescription business being run by a drop-out who enjoyed concocting his own medicines.

So Doc talked Daddy into moving to Rowja to run the business. Daddy had served in the Navy for the tail end of World War II and then graduated from pharmacy school at The University. He'd been working in Louisiana at the time and his new wife, the "city girl," was none too thrilled about moving "to the woods." But, after a stern, whither thou go-est lecture from one of her great aunts, move she did. Truth be known, she was even less thrilled about moving next door to her in-laws, but that's a story for another time.

So, they packed up nearly 'bout a hundred years of history and merchandise and moved it to Rowja. They thought about changing the name of the store, but it just didn't seem right. So the new McRiley's carries on with Doc as McRiley's honorary druggist and good will ambassador, and follows the tradition of having everything anybody in a small town might need. We even still have a soda fountain. And, that's where we were headed.

When we got to the store, Doc was plum tickled to see Sister. Mama looked up from helping a customer, crossed her eyes and stuck out her tongue. The sales clerks all hollered greetings. Daddy said that he'd be with us in a minute. He was typing a prescription label.

We went on back to the fountain where Annie asked Sister what she'd have. She didn't have to ask me. I would be having two hot dogs with mayonnaise, a bag of Fritos, and a vanilla malt.

"I don't know. I'm kind of torn between the Frito pie and the salad plate."

You would be hard pressed to find less healthy meals than a Frito pie, my traditional meal, or a McRiley's salad plate.

A Frito pie is a bag of Fritos that you cut open down the front to make a pouch. Then you pour in about a cup of Wolf Brand Chili and top that with grated up cheddar cheese and some chopped up onions. You could pour on some nacho cheese if you were of a mind, but McRiley's used grated up cheese that was left over from slicing up the cheese for cheeseburgers. If you're really feeling festive, and Sister usually was, you sprinkle Tabasco on top of the onions.

Now given all that, you might think a salad plate would be a good choice, but a McRiley's salad plate might not be what you expect. Our mama invented the salad plate for all those folks who were trying to watch their diet. It seemed like every member of every women's society in town (Garden, Music, Quilting, you name it) would come in at least once a week for a salad plate. The salad plate is:

A scoop each of your favorite salads
Egg Salad, Chicken Salad, Tuna Fish Salad, and
Pimento Cheese Salad
Substitute Pear Salad (in season)
Served with Club Crackers and butter.

I probably ought to tell you that each of these salads had about twice as much mayonnaise as my hot dogs. Also, the pears in the pear salad were canned. "In season" had to do with whether they were on sale down at Mr. Baker's grocery.

"I guess I'll go with the Frito pie."

"Annie, I'll have me a hamburger." Doc walked up and took a seat at the counter.

"Doc, do you suppose you could get Mama and Daddy to have a bite with us? I've got a project I need to tell y'all about."

Doc shook his head and chuckled, "I imagine so." Sister was known for her projects. "Your daddy's near 'bout finished with the nursing home order and your mama was up there cussing and trying to help Miz Williams figure out the lipstick colors. Somebody tore off some of the labels and they're having a time going on about Royal Red as opposed to Ruby Red. I'll be back afore my burger's off the griddle."

Sure enough, before I'd made it through my second dog, the three of them came wandering back.

"Now, what's this project?"

The Big House

"The project is for Summester, and I need the big house, so we'll have a place to stay." Sister explained.

Sister went to a small college over in Louisiana called Althea College. It was the school Mama's people attended. Daddy had always said that no child of his was ever going to private school, but it was a family school, and she got a pretty good-sized scholarship, so that helped change his mind. Because it was a private school, it could get away with doing some things differently than other colleges.

Most places around here had two main semesters and then some sort of summer session where you could get ahead if you wanted to or catch up if you'd messed up. Fall semester started toward the end of August and got out about the middle of December. Spring semester would start about the middle of January and get out in the middle of May. Then they'd stick a summer semester between spring and fall.

Not Althea. The folks there believed in a "more personalized learning environment." Daddy said they took a perfectly reasonable schedule and squoze in some extra tuition opportunities.

It had two main semesters just like normal. Where it got strange was by not starting spring semester until about February 1. January became Intermester. During Intermester you took one subject, but you studied it every day for 5 or 6 hours for about three weeks. Mind you, these weren't exactly standard classes like French or World History or Chemistry or something like that. I looked at the list one time, and it was classes like "Prefixes, Suffixes, and Roots in Legal and Medical Terminology," "Romance Literature of the Middle East," "John Philip Sousa and the Politics of Marching Bands." You get the idea. That's Intermester, and it means that spring semester didn't let out until about June 1.

Althea had a regular kind of summer semester with normal kinds of classes, but it also had something called Summester. In Summester, you came up with a project to do on your own or in a small group. You'd have to get a professor to agree to work on the project with you, but once you did, you were on your way.

Students were required to take at least three Intermesters or Summesters. It didn't matter if you took three Intermesters and no Summesters or three Summesters and no Intermesters or two of one and one of the other, but you had to take three. You could get out of one, and only one by going on a college sponsored trip to another country, but that was it.

Sister had been on a trip and had done an Intermester. She had purely hated going to one class for all that time in a row even if she could now win any battle of Name that Tune so long as it involved a Broadway musical from before the 1970s. So we'd known all along that a Summester was coming even if we didn't quite know what it'd be.

They didn't get a normal spring break either. Instead of a week like everybody else, they'd get Monday, Tuesday, and Wednesday of Mardi Gras week off and then, almost forty days later, they'd get Maundy Thursday and Good Friday of Holy Week off.

Like I said, it's weird, but so is Sister.

Doc sighed, "Okay what are we going to have to do?" Sister was notorious for getting us all roped in to working on her projects. The fact that it wasn't due the next day was a bit of a surprise to all of us. She was also notorious for procrastination.

About that time, Me-Mama walked in the back door and joined us at one of the ice cream tables.

"I was headed home and thought I saw your car," she said.

The extent to which my grandmother would have had to go out of her way to see Sister's car at the store may be worth pointing out. She would have had to head about two miles in the opposite direction of her house. More likely was that the next client of the Spritz and Shine had seen Sister's car. Then when Me-Mama got home and nobody was there, she figured out where we were.

"I'm glad you came in. I was just about to tell y'all about our Summester project. Is it okay if we open up the big house?"

"Well, I guess so," Me-Mama allowed—after all it was her people's home place—"but why would you want to do that?"

Truth be known, the big house was probably smaller than either of the houses we live in now, but it was the big house when it was built, and that's what we all still call it.

Me-Mama's daddy—we call him Papa—and a couple of his brothers settled with their parents in what is now Rayburn County in about 1877. They had come over from Alabama and Mississippi after The War to rebuild their lives. Land was cheap, and they bought as much as they could, and they kept buying it over the years. They mostly raised cotton and cattle and eventually owned a big chunk of the land in the north and western parts of the county. A little bit pokes up into the county just north of us.

Papa willed each of his children about the same amount of land–a few hundred acres. Me-Mama's property was the southernmost, and our houses were located on the highway between Mayhaw and Rowja. Much to Mama's dismay, they were right next to one another with only a dirt road in between.

The dirt road was a shortcut to the home place where the big house is located. It's not very far as the crow flies, but you have to drive a right fair piece to get there due to creeks and bottom land that doesn't require a gully washer to flood.

Anyhow, the dirt road between our houses leads to a farm-to-market road that you turn right on. The farm-to-market road eventually winds its way to just outside of Hannibal, the county seat of the country to the north and Rowja's bitterest rival in everything. You do not want to go to Hannibal. About seven miles down the farm-to-market road, there's a turn-off to the right. You can recognize the turn because if you look off to the right you can see Woodrock Baptist Church sitting on top of a hill. Sometimes there's a sign, sometimes there's not, so don't count on a sign. Turn right again. Just beyond the church, there's a place where five roads come together. About all that's left at the crossroads is a volunteer fire department. Most of the firefighters are kin to us and most of the fires they fight are at kinfolks' places. Used to be though, there was a general store, a school house where my grandmother and her brothers and sisters took schooling, and the Woodrock Post Office. Woodrock was named when Papa and his brothers uncovered big pieces of a petrified tree when they were trying to clear a field.

If you turn left at the crossroad, you head to the Methodist church and the Woodrock cemetery. Head straight across and eventually you'll come out just above Mayhaw. Turn right and you'll dead end after a while at the old gin. Take a hard right turn that almost doubles back on itself and you wind up on a twisting winding dirt road. It's a good dirt road though, so you don't have to worry much about getting stuck unless nobody's tended to the beaver dam for a while. As you go along, the main dirt road will branch off into a spider web of smaller roads that crisscross much of what used to be Papa's property. Just keep winding down the main dirt road about four or five miles until you see a nice farm house directly ahead of you. That's the big house on the home place.

It was a whole lot easier to tell people how to get there before somebody moved the couch. A couch had been dumped on the side of the road in a big curve about one-and-a-half miles from the crossroad. It was right easy to say "just go about three-and-a-half miles past the couch." People would look at you funny, but they'd see what you meant and not worry that they'd gone down the wrong road or something. Granddaddy said it was a terrible thing when the county finally picked up that couch.

Papa willed the home place and the land around it to his daughter Catherine, one of the Catherines for whom my sister is *not* named. Papa did this because Catherine was the daughter who took care of the household after his wife died giving birth to Me-Mama. She then nursed him and ran the farm after he got sick with whatever it was that killed him. All we ever heard was that it was some sort of wasting disease. Papa also wanted to make sure that Aunt Catherine was taken care of because her husband, my Uncle Poodle, wasn't exactly the most reliable fellow you'd ever hope to meet. He was nice enough, but didn't have any interest in farming.

Papa and his wife were ahead of their time in some ways. They expected all their children to get an education. Once they'd finished school, then they were expected to work on the property, get married, or go to college. At least four of the girls, including Aunt Catherine and Me-Mama, went to college. Aunt Catherine met Uncle Poodle when she was at college in Nacogdoches. Uncle Poodle, whose name was really Bob France, was a handsome fellow who played third base and pitched for the local semi-pro baseball team. Aunt Catherine met him, they fell in love, and got married before her first year of school was done and before anybody back home knew it had happened. Papa sent Me-Mama to school in Huntsville when it came time for her to head off.

Anyhow, Aunt Catherine came home while Uncle Poodle traveled all over East Texas and neighboring states playing ball for semi-pro and minor league teams. He even got to play in the major leagues for a little while. Playing in the major leagues made him nervous, though, and he'd drink himself back to the minors. His playing career was interrupted when he was filled with patriotism and headed off to fight the Kaiser. His drinking went on uninterrupted. It wasn't that he was a mean drunk or anything. It was just that after the Great War he was pretty well washed up as a ballplayer, and farm life bored him. He started staying away more and more.

Granddaddy always said that he enjoyed Poodle's company whenever he was around. They'd sit out on the porch smoking cigars, drinking brown liquor from prescription bottles, and telling stories about how things were and weren't. Daddy allowed as to how Uncle Poodle was the only reason he had any athletic success at all. Our granddaddy worked at the store all day nearly 'bout every day, but when he was home, Uncle Poodle didn't much work. Instead, he would come into town and throw the ball, or shoot a basketball, or punt a football, or hit a tennis ball. Uncle Poodle was quite the athlete.

Uncle Poodle left Woodrock and Aunt Catherine for good about ten years before I was born. I met him once that I can remember, and he taught me how to throw a curve ball. I thought he was the best. He and Aunt Catherine didn't have any children that lived, and they never got divorced. Me-Mama said they always loved each other, but they just couldn't stand one another.

Uncle Poodle died a few years back, and Aunt Catherine followed not long after. She left the home place and the land around it to Me-Mama. There were howls of protest from the descendants of her other brothers and sisters during the reading of the will. But years of running the farm and dealing with all of Uncle Poodle's foolishness had turned Aunt Catherine into a clear-thinking business woman. Nobody knew if she left it all to Me-Mama because she was the baby, or because she thought one of Me-Mama's grandchildren was named for her, or because my granddaddy or daddy had periodically given her work at the store when money was tight, or because Doc was one of the few people in the family who genuinely liked Poodle. Whatever the reason, the home place belonged to Me-Mama, and Sister wanted to use it.

The Project

"Two questions," Daddy said. "What is this project and who is we?"

"The project is to write an oral history of the county. A group of us that have or had family here is going to tell how our families got here and how they lived back when until now. It's an ethnography."

Granddaddy allowed to how anything that ended in "ography" had something to do with taxes or maps. Either that or it was a Latin word meaning "too much education."

Sister ignored Granddaddy. "How much do you want to know?"

"Not much," Mama said. "Other than are we going to have to do anything?"

"Not really. We'll probably want to interview you and some other folks, but that'll be about it. Just family stories about things that went on. We'll combine that with info from old issues of the *Stampede* and the *Trumpet* and whatever records we can find at the courthouse and churches. Some folks may even have some old diaries or something. We're mainly just trying to write the story of our people."

The *Trumpet* and the *Stampede* were the newspapers in the county. The *Trumpet*, "covering the news 'til Gabriel calls," had been located in Mayhaw. The *Stampede*, "rounding up all the news," is in Rowja. Sadly, the *Trumpet* did not stick around for Gabriel. Ted Wilford sold it to the *Stampede* a while back, so now we have the *Trumpet Stampede*, a name that sounds like a bad start to a halftime show. Its motto is "rounding up the news 'til Gabriel calls."

"Who assigned this thing?"

"Well, we picked it out ourselves, but we're writing it for Dr. Byrd in Southern History and Culture. She's real excited about the project."

"Oh, Renee Byrd. I used to date her husband, L.P. We may have even been engaged. I can't exactly remember."

Before she met my Daddy, Mama was a serial dater who had several engagements. Her personal philosophy was, "They're not taken until they're dead."

"She's so nice." Mama said. "I just love it when we sit together at the games. We just talk and talk about L.P."

"Yes, and I was particularly thrilled when he announced to everyone within hearing distance that if things had been a little different I would have been his child. That's just what you want to hear from the Registrar."

Doc piped up. "You know Ted Wilford's storehouse burnt up, don't you? A trash fire got out of hand. You might have some trouble finding old copies of the *Trumpet*. I don't know where he kept 'em."

Me-Mama said, "I think they have some copies down to the museum, but I'll bet you that Effie has copies of everything out in her shed."

Effie Floyd was a local legend. She was nigh onto a hundred years old and had worked on and off at one or another of our newspapers since the Roosevelt administration, Teddy, not Franklin, as Grandaddy was quick to point out. Effie still wrote a weekly column for the *Trumpet Stampede*. She mostly just reported on whoever had called her that week to say their garden was coming in or that they had folks visiting from out of town.

She didn't much get out of the house anymore except to go to church, get her hair done, grocery shop, or eat at the New New Mexican Restaurant for the monthly meeting of the 90+ Society. The New New Mexican restaurant is on the Square. The first Mexican restaurant, the Mexican Restaurant, is out Mayhaw highway. The second Mexican restaurant, the New Mexican Restaurant, is between the Square and the cemetery near the railroad tracks. The New New Mexican Restaurant was the third to open. Those aren't really their names, but all their true names start with El and the second word starts with Po—Poblano, Pollo, Pollito—it was just easier our way.

You can always recognize Effie driving around. Maybe I should say you can always recognize Effie's car. You can't really see her other than a tuft of jet black hair and signs of a forehead between the top of the steering wheel and the dashboard.

It is generally understood that Effie has the right-of-way regardless of stop signs, traffic lights, or one-way streets. It's pretty easy to do because she keeps such a predictable schedule. Every so often she'll cross us up, but mostly she sticks to her route. We just go another way.

She drives this big old black Lincoln Continental at roughly fourteen miles an hour. She also brakes abruptly if she sees any sort of threat to her personal safety—another car, children playing in a sprinkler, a dog on a porch, a hill, or a curve. This means that if you find yourself behind her, you should try hard not to exceed twelve miles an hour lest she slam on the brakes and you slam into her.

An accident with Effie causes bad things. First, it's your fault. Second, hitting the Lincoln at that speed will damage your car and will not cause a mark to appear on hers. Third, Effie will put your name in the paper and not be nice about it. Like I said, Effie gets the right-of-way.

"Miz Floyd's a great idea. We should probably interview her, too. She knows more about county history than anyone."

"Just take a lot of batteries," said Me-Mama. Miz Floyd was bad to run on. "You also might give the library a try."

"Really?" Sister was not convinced.

"I don't see why she should bother. Last I checked Rayburn County had not appeared anywhere in the *Reader's Digest Condensed Books* or *Highlights for Children*," Granddaddy claimed.

He made a good point. A lot of the books and magazines had come from things that didn't sell at yard sales and from whatever the doctors didn't want in their waiting rooms anymore. That accounts for why there were a couple dozen or so copies of that blue-covered *First Bible Book* in the library's children section.

"Now, Doc, you know it's gotten better ever since the Lions Club made it a project," said Me-Mama. "They even hired nice Mr. Julian to be a librarian."

"Well, I wouldn't get my hopes up. You're probably going to have better luck with Effie. At least she's probably got everything organized. It's going to take Julian a spell to sort through that tumble."

Daddy broke in, "Okay, so you and some of your school friends are going to live at the big house this summer while you interview folks and dig through old papers." Daddy was getting anxious about prescriptions piling up even though the other pharmacist seemed to be handling things. "And your scholarship covers the tuition, and you won't need room and board at the school."

"Right. The only expenses will be the electric and gas at the big house, and I can ask everybody to chip in for that," offered Sister.

"Oh, don't worry about that, Sister. I imagine the house will enjoy the company," Me-Mama said. "We'll get the power turned on at the pole and make sure the water pump's working."

"You'll probably want to eat sometime, too. We'll whup up a meal or two." Doc added.

"That'd be mighty fine. So we can use the big house?"

Me-Mama, Doc, Mama, and Daddy all looked around at each other, nodded and shrugged. "It ought to work."

"Now for my second question. Who all is coming?" Daddy tried again.

"And, can any of you shoot a gun?" added Doc.

The Group

"Doc, for heaven's sake, they don't need a gun!" Me-Mama was flabbergasted.

"There's a lot of meanness about, and I don't like the idea of a bunch of girls out in the woods. It is all girls, isn't it?"

"Yes sir."

"Peter and Pauline are right there, and Peter would durn sure die himself before he'd let anything happen to them," insisted Me-Mama.

Peter and Pauline lived at the bottom of the hill just outside the gate to the big house. Peter was one of Mama's strays. Mama collected people like Daddy collected animals. Some folks said that Peter had been dropped on his head as a baby. Mama allowed as to how she just didn't think his bread was quite done.

Don't get me wrong. Peter is a great guy. He just can't really hold down a normal job or concentrate on things like the alphabet for very long. Mama tried to have him work at the store for a while as a stock clerk, but he had a problem putting things in the right place.

The worst was the time he mixed the KY jelly in amongst the Dento-Grip. An old lady, I won't call her name, who didn't see real well and was too proud to wear her glasses, was aiming for the Dento-Grip and came out with the jelly. She didn't notice until the next day when her teeth purely refused to stay in her mouth. Mama didn't so much get mad at Peter as she wanted to know why the sales clerk hadn't asked if that was really what the woman wanted. The sales clerk's reasoning was that it wasn't the sort of thing that you asked about. The woman might have been feeling optimistic.

Mama couldn't fire Peter, so she told him he was being transferred to another office. The office turned out to be the "little" house—a tenant house that Mama had updated. His new title was full-time security officer. Mama paid him some and didn't charge rent. He started out by watching over the place and doing some general maintenance.

Peter attended the Baptist church at Woodrock because Me-Mama told him to. That's where he met Pauline, one of our cousins. It was love at first sight for both of them. The wedding was at the Woodrock church, and the preacher made it a point to note that it was just fittin' and proper that two folks named Peter and Pauline had gotten together. He confined his readings to the New Testament in their honor.

As it turns out, Peter is a genius at hunting and fishing and can fix near 'bout anything if you aren't too particular about when it gets done or what it winds up looking like. He earns some money by claiming bounties on feral hogs tearing up people's places. But, the most amazing thing he does is guide high-end fishing tours up all these little sloughs and bayous. The boy can find some fish, so now all these professional athletes like Cowboys and Rangers and Astros and such make their way to the little house to contract with Peter to help negotiate the area. Mama was always thankful Pauline had the sense to charge for his services and to make sure folks paid. Otherwise they might have taken advantage of his sweet nature.

Pauline was talented in her own right. She did fine needlework and all sorts of sewing. Mama and Me-Mama agreed that it would be a promising opportunity if they opened a business in the little house and continued to live there. It was a proud day when Peter and Pauline cut the ribbon in front of the new sign Doc had painted to replace the HomePlace Security sign. Good News Fish and Upholstery was open for business. As a grand opening present, Me-Mama deeded Peter and Pauline the little house and five acres around and behind it including road access all the way down to Taterhead Creek.

No, Peter wouldn't let anything happen to the girls.

"Let's get *back* to the question. Who all is going to be staying at the house?" Daddy tried once again.

"It's not completely settled," said Sister, "but I know most everybody who'll be here. You probably know most of them or their people. First off, Winnie Clifton, of course."

Smiles and laughter erupted around the table. Sister and Winnie Clifton had been best friends since they were toddlers. They went through elementary, middle, and junior high school together even though Winnie was almost a year older. She'd missed the cut-off for starting school the year before my sister barely made it. So they started together.

They would play like characters from TV and movies, have sleepovers, ride bicycles, sing in the choir, play in the band, and, well, the long and the short of it was that you hardly ever saw one without the other. At least that was the case until that terrible day when Winnie Clifton's daddy got promoted and transferred to the main office of the lumber company he'd worked for. They had to move down to Houston.

Sister and Winnie made a pact that they would always be best friends, and they held to it. It didn't hurt a bit that Winnie's mama and our mama were best friends, too, so they helped keep the connection going. Sister would spend a couple of weeks every summer with the Cliftons in Houston and Winnie would stay a couple of weeks with us. They'd go off to church camp every year—the Methodist one—they claimed the Baptist camp was boring and weird because they weren't allowed to be anywhere near the boys. Naturally, Winnie and Sister worked it out to go to the same college. About the only thing they didn't do was take the same classes. Winnie majored in religious studies, and Sister majored in whatever struck her fancy that semester. Daddy just hoped she'd graduate despite herself.

"Susie B. is coming for sure."

"Susanna Beatrice Burton?!" Me-Mama was surprised.

"One of those Burtons staying at our place? That's mighty high cotton," Granddaddy snorted.

The Burtons were the closest thing that Rowja had to founding fathers or, really, a founding mother. They'd been among the first Americans to be anywhere around Rowja. In fact, Susie B.'s great-something-or-another grandmother is credited with naming Rowja and preventing a war. (I'll tell you more about that later.)

"Susie B. grew up in Fort Worth, so she's not near as snotty as the ones around here."

"That's a blessing."

"And she goes by Susie B. She just ignores that whole Beatrice part."

I need to tell you how to pronounce her name in case you come to East Texas. It's Bee-AT-trice, like there's a BEE AT a town called TRICE and trice rhymes with (I won't say what Granddaddy usually says) . . . hiss. Now, I know that there's people who call themselves Bee-uh-trice especially over in England, but that's just not how we say it and people will look at you funny if you do. And, whatever you do, don't try to correct the way they say their own or their mama's or grandmama's pronunciation of Beatrice. It's not polite and will not be appreciated.

"Lee Harris hasn't decided if she's coming yet."

"Well, bless her heart, you can't rightly blame her," Granddaddy allowed.

Around Rowja, the name Lee Harris was often followed by "bless her heart." It was almost like it was her last name, Lee Harris Blessherheart. Lee didn't live in Rowja, but a lot of her people were still here, so she and her family made right regular visits.

Lee was named for her granddaddy's sister, Robertie Lee Harris. You've heard tell of her as Bertie, and, yes, Bertie was named for the general.

Anyhow, you can probably understand why people are quick to bless her heart and why Lee Harris might not be all that eager to spend a summer in Rowja.

"I'm thinking she'll join us," Sister said. "She's real interested in the project and doesn't have anything lined up or even thought up. Besides, it's not like she'd actually have to stay with Bertie."

"Heavens no."

"Vera Harwich is absolutely in."

"Oh dear, will she be wearing black all summer?" Mama asked.

"I'm not so much wondering about that as what color her hair's going to be," Daddy added.

Granddaddy was completely confused. "Who is Vera Harwich?"

Mama piped in, "She lives in Sister's dorm. You don't know her, but her grandmama and granddaddy are Will and Ida Miller up on the hill between here and Mayhaw. Ethel's girl"

Ethel Miller had gone off to work at the ammunition plant outside of Bossier City during the war. She'd bus out to the plant every day from an apartment she shared with some other girls from Mayhaw. During this time, she met an airman stationed at Barksdale. They had a whirlwind romance and married before he shipped out. Her family was most distressed because he was a Yankee and a Republican to boot. After the war, he collected her and they went off to live in one of those states that start with the letter "I". They sent Vera to school down South because she wanted to get away and because she could do that and still have family nearby.

"Now that I know who she is, what about her hair?"

"She's a drama major."

"Oh, well, as long as she's not a Republican."

"The last one is Merril Reynolds."

"Now, I don't know any Reynolds," said Me-Mama, "Who are her people?"

"I don't think any of them live here. She doesn't know a thing about whether her family had anything to do with Rowja other than this picture she found. It's an old postcard photograph of a young man standing in front of what I think looks like our courthouse. The back of the card says, 'Finally in Texas . . . I'm a real cowboy now.' The postmark is blurred out like it got wet, but it's addressed to her great-grandmother or maybe an aunt. I forget. They found it when they were cleaning out an old trunk."

"So why is she working on this project?"

"To tell you the truth. I think Dr. Byrd feels a little sorry for her. She's down here by herself and needs a Summester project. She's nice enough, but kind of odd. Dr. Byrd said she could look at the history more objectively than we could."

"Where's she from?"

"Some little town outside Buffalo, New York."

"Good Lord, we're going to have a half-Yankee and a full-Yankee staying at the big house. Your papa is going to spin himself until he hits oil," Granddaddy pretended to swoon.

"Now, be nice," Me-Mama said, always the planner, "That ought to be just fine. Two can stay in Mama and Papa's room, two can stay in the boys' room and two can stay in the girls' room."

"Oh, and I was wondering if Speedy would want to join us."

Everyone was surprised, especially Speedy. I know because I'm Speedy. I got the name from my cousin's husband, my elementary school principal. He named me Speedy because, well, I'm not. The name stuck.

"It would be nice to have someone who could take the riding mower on errands and to help us keep things organized and take notes."

"So I'd be a secretary? Thank you kindly, no."

"What if you wouldn't miss any games, and I could talk Doc out of your summer chores? And you know the Astros games come in clearer on the radio out there."

Doc laughed. "We might could work something out. That's a whole lot less than you normally need me to do on one of your projects."

Suddenly, I was a lot more interested in the Summester project. Doc's summer chores were terrible and mainly designed to make sure that his grandchildren planned on going to college. One of the easier chores was balancing on hay bales stacked in the back of Doc's truck as he bounced his way across the pasture to feed the cows. The job was to cut the baling wire and kick or shove the bale off the moving truck without following it yourself.

A medium hard chore was walking the fence lines and fixing places that had broken. That doesn't sound so bad, but there are miles of fences that you just can't get to. So you have to tote barb wire, nails, wire clippers, and all sorts of stuff. Plus, even though it's 100 degrees you have to wear boots, heavy long pants, a long sleeve shirt, and thick leather gloves due to the poison everything, blackberry vines, ticks, chiggers, and snakes.

The worst chores had to do with working the chicken houses. From the time they arrive on their baby chick school busses until they go to their greater reward, it is one nasty job after the next until you finally have to clean out the houses after they're gone. I'd tell you more about it, but you might not ever want to eat chicken again and that would be bad for business.

"Well, where would Speedy stay?" Me-Mama was still in full blown planning.

"How 'bout the sleeping porch?"

That sealed it. The sleeping porch, spending time with Sister and her friends, listening to games, and getting out of Doc's chores had the makings of the best summer ever. "I'd be glad to help if it's all right with everyone."

It was settled. Mama and Daddy went back to work. Doc went back to doing whatever he wanted to, and Me-Mama continued to quiz Sister about her friends. I went to read comics. It was fine with Mama and Daddy because as long as I kept them nice, I could put them back in the rack as soon as I was done.

Later Sister told me she didn't mind the inquisition because she'd already told her friends they'd be able to use the big house and had counted on it being okay. Truth be told, Me-Mama probably already knew that. She had developed mind-reading abilities over her fifty-some-odd years of teaching elementary school. Even so, it was nice that everything was official.

Wrong Damn Funeral

Sister and I spent the next few days fluffing the big house and getting ready for her friends to arrive. We opened up the windows and aired out the rooms so it wouldn't smell musty when we turned on the air. We changed the sheets and washed and dried a bizarre variety of towels and washrags. Zeus roamed the house making sure that no unwelcome critters had moved in since the family had gathered for Easter. He didn't find anything worth mentioning. We rinsed off the plates, glasses, and cookware, changed the paper in the cabinets and put everything back. We loaded the refrigerator with the necessities of life. Finally, we washed windows, dusted, swept, mopped, vacuumed, and generally tidied.

It wasn't all that bad because it would just keep us from having to do it later in the summer before the family reunion and dinner on the grounds. Fluffing the big house for the reunion, Christmas, and other occasions was one of Doc's lesser chores because, for the most part, you were in a heated or cooled building and because you were not as likely to come across something dead.

The morning before the Altheans were to arrive, Sister and I were running late for lunch over at Me-Mama's house due to a last second fluffing emergency. We had neglected to put the Co-Colas in the icebox. When we got to Me-Mama's house, we weren't in trouble because nobody was eating. Me-Mama, Aunt MiMi (short for Naomi), Uncle Pat and Aunt Lucy were just sitting around. Granddaddy was nowhere to be seen. It was already 11:30 and pretty soon Uncle Pat would be complaining about how his stomach was going to think his throat had been cut.

Before either of us could say anything, MiMi blurted out, "That's right. We're slap starved to death but your granddaddy has gone to a funeral, and we're waiting on him." Our granddaddy was MiMi's baby brother and had tormented her in one way or another for more than seventy years.

Granddaddy did love a funeral and attended as many as he could. He said folks appreciated it, and besides, if he went to a lot of funerals then maybe a lot of people would come to his.

Me-Mama allowed to as how the funeral started at 10:00 and she was surprised it was taking so long. It was for old man Wilson who didn't have hardly any people at all and was so old that nobody much even remembered him. But before he'd gone to the nursing home, he'd been a good customer at the store. Being a good customer meant that he'd generally paid his bills more or less on time. Me-Mama said that the crowd must have been so small that Granddaddy had gone to the graveside lest he had stood out for not being there.

Before my sister could make a comment about standing out by being absent, Granddaddy came barging through the screen door.

"Doc, where've you been? We're sitting here planning our own services on account of having starved." MiMi tended to speak her mind.

"You hush your mouth. I gotta to go to the bathroom and then we'll eat. I can't see you starving between now and Labor Day no how. "

"Doc, that ole bad man's gonna get you."

Granddaddy was gone for a good long while when Me-Mama headed down the hall saying, "I'm gonna go check on him."

Me-Mama was gone for a fair while herself when Uncle Pat began to complain about whatever was going on. Aunt Lucy wondered if the ole bad man had actually gotten him, and Aunt MiMi allowed to as how she thought there must be a bear or something back there.

Sister said, "Shoot a mile," stood up, and set out to check when the two of them came back up the hall—Granddaddy being mighty quiet, and Me-Mama smirking and shaking her head.

"Doc, pray and let's eat the blessing," MiMi roared.

After the blessing, Granddaddy was oddly quiet, meaning he was quiet at all. Finally, he shook his head and said, "Y'all aren't going to believe this, but I went to the wrong damn funeral."

"Doc, you swore me not to tell."

"I know, but I just can't keep it in."

Then everybody took to asking whose funeral it was and how it was that he came to be at the wrong one.

"Well, I just don't know. I figured old man Wilson's funeral would be at Rose Haven, so that's where I went. Turns out he was at Jackson's."

"Jackson's?"

It was easy enough to be confused. Almost nobody had a funeral at Jackson's Mortuary and Funereal Arts unless they happened to be Jacksons or Jackson-in-laws.

"I never knew he was a Jackson."

"I don't think he was. I think with everything going on, Rose Haven was just booked solid. They must have sent old man Wilson over to Jackson's so they could get him in the ground."

"Well, whose funeral did you go to?"

"It was right peculiar. I got to the funeral home not long before the services because I didn't figure there'd be a problem finding a seat. But the place was just packed, and there were all these young girls just weeping and wailing. I had to get right in the line to view the body before I could even look for a seat. I was sneaking looks out of the corner of my eye and didn't hardly know a soul. I drew the conclusion that old man Wilson must have had a lot of out-of-town kin who thought he had money. Anyways, when I got up to the casket and looked, it weren't old man Wilson."

"Who was it?" said Sister.

"I didn't rightly know. Some young feller. I didn't recognize him even though people kept talking about how natural he looked and what a good job they'd done with him. So I sniffled and worked up a tear before I went back to find a seat. I thought about trying to slip out the back, but wouldn't you know I ran into Miz McConkey."

The entire room sighed. Miz McConkey considered herself quite the conversationalist. My sister would point out that conversational skills usually didn't include lengthy soliloquies about every bunion, flat tire, burnt cornbread, or other misfortune that ever befell her or a member of her family. It was a matter of some dispute whether it was better to be stuck with Miz McConkey, Effie Floyd, or Bertie.

"It was good in a way because she knew what was going on, and I didn't have to play like I did because she didn't take a lot of breaths. Turns out the departed was one of her kinfolks from Reeb."

To my family, saying someone was from Reeb was right up there with calling them no-account. Reeb was right on the river and named by the family of outlaws that settled there. They didn't actually pick Reeb for the name. They originally named it to honor their favorite family activity, but when they went to register it, the post office wouldn't let them use it. So, they reversed the letters. A lot of the citizens of Reeb carried on in the great tradition of their ancestors. Granddaddy often pointed out that much of East Texas was settled by folks on the run from the law what with it being just across the border from France, then Spain, then France again, and then finally America. He would add that folks from Reeb were not only outlaws, they were lazy outlaws because they just barely made it across the water. A posse could still shoot at them if they were so inclined.

"Well, he was from Reeb, but he seems to have been a fine fellow. He was on the ball teams and went to University Interscholastic League in number sense. She gave me his whole history. He was even looking at a scholarship."

"Heavenly days, what happened?"

"Nobody really knows. He had a motorcycle wreck, but there doesn't seem to be a reason. It was a clear day, no other cars around. McConkey says he was a safe driver, and he was wearing a helmet. The police don't even seem to think he was going too fast. The best anybody can figure is that he swerved to miss some animal in the road."

"How was the service?"

"It was right odd. They had tape recorded music."

"Oh dear. That is unfortunate."

My people did not consider tape recorded music to be acceptable at a funeral, wedding, or church service. I'm not sure why. Maybe it was some sort of character flaw if you couldn't manage to come up with people to sing and play the piano.

There was an exception to this rule. Cousin Jessie sang at just about every wedding and funeral our family ever had, so when she was killed in a car wreck a few years back, it just seemed right that they played a tape of her singing. I admit it was peculiar, but she did have a real pretty voice. Now, you often hear a tape of Jessie playing at family events. I guess the rule should be amended to say that tape recorded music by family members was all right, but that tape recorded music by perfect strangers was no account.

"Well, it just figures that people from Reeb would go and do that."

"What all did they play?"

"Oh, you know that new music where they just holler over a bunch of noise. One song had a bunch of water and seagull sounds, and the feller kept going on sayin' 'I'm your captain'."

"Grand Funk Railroad?" Sister exclaimed.

"Melanie Catherine!" Aunt Lucy, who didn't hear real well, was shocked.

Before Sister could explain, Granddaddy went on saying that the preacher had tied the song to being the captain of his soul. "Which I found tacky," he added, "because if the boy had steered better . . ."

"Doc, I suwannee," Me-Mama interrupted.

"Anyhow, it wasn't too long before Bertie started carrying on again about angels, the hand of God, sins of the fathers—just like she did at Tommy Austin's funeral except that a bunch of them big ole fellers from Reeb just picked her up and packed her right on out of there."

"That's a shame. Seems like we've had a lot of young'uns go recently. Some folks act like they ain't got good sense. Now, you two need to watch yourselves. You know people die in threes."

"Yes'm, MiMi," Sister and I mumbled, and wondered which of us MiMi thought was doomed.

As we were saying our good-byes, we heard Granddaddy arguing, "Naomi, three people have already died—Tommy Austin, old man Wilson, and the boy from Reeb."

"Doc, you know old man Wilson doesn't count."

"I don't know why not. He's just as dead as the others."

We left quietly while we had the chance.

The Project Begins

After lunch, we headed on back to the big house to await the arrival of the group. Winnie Clifton was the first to get there. Of course, she knew the way and wasn't distracted by all the possible side roads. Susie B. drove up next, followed closely by Lee. Vera and Merril rode together from the college on account of Merril not having a car. Each arrival was marked by a major celebration even through they'd all been together at school not more than ten days before.

Vera was particularly impressive being "exhausted" and "famished" from her "journey." Sister pointed out that her journey was a little more than an hour and that they'd passed two Dairy Queens and a Sonic between there and here. Even so, it was Co-Colas and MiMi's homemade teacakes all around. I was introduced to the group as its chief assistant.

The Altheans spent the rest of the afternoon getting situated and exploring the house and the grounds. Buddy and Lady were also staying with us to act as "*detergents*;" Mama sometimes got words mixed up. Fierce beasts that they were, they were enjoying the attention being lavished upon them.

Merril was particularly impressed about Catherine's and her sister's and her mama's quilting and tatting that was displayed throughout the house. Apparently, her family had worked with some sort of craft guild up in New York. In fact, she said that the fellow in the picture, "the real cowboy," had left the guild when its founder and his wife had gone down with the Lusitania when it was torpedoed. Her ancestor, she wasn't quite sure of his name, had decided that the place was going to pieces, and he'd up and left for Texas. The nature of his departure was a scandal on the family, and he was practically disowned. The guild survived, and the rest of Merril's family had stayed and made a go of it. The postcard was the last they'd heard from him.

"Did you bring the card?" Susie B. asked.

"Give me a moment." Merril went to her suitcases and rummaged through some papers. "Here it is."

"Well, you can't see much of it, but what you can see sure looks like our courthouse," Sister allowed. "Winnie, what do you think?"

"Sure enough, but remember Hannibal had a twin to it. They tore theirs down to put up something less . . ."

"Creepy?" Vera offered.

It was true that the Rayburn County Courthouse looked spooky. It and the one in the hated Hannibal had been designed by an immigrant from the old country to look like the castles of his homeland. His childhood neighbors on either side must have been the Counts Dracula and Frankenstein. It even had thirteen fireplaces and chimneys to make it scarier.

"That too, but the county Hannibal is in is on the edge of the East Texas Oil Field, and they had the money to build a more modern facility."

"It's way less cool," I piped in, defending Rowja's honor.

"That is so true." Winnie came to my support. "Hannibal's just looks like some sort of blockhouse. Rowja's courthouse is unique."

"It doesn't look quite so gothic when you realize it's made out of red brick. This old photo just makes it look gray."

"And foreboding," Vera added.

"There's a hanging tree," I tried to add interest.

"Oh, goody." Vera made a disgusted face.

"Nonetheless, I say that this postcard provides evidence that Merril has a connection to Rowja and that she's officially a member of this project."

"Wasn't I anyway?"

"Certainly, but now we can claim in the paper's introduction that all the members of the group have family ties to the area." Winnie always had a goal in mind.

"Has anybody thought about how we're going to carry out this project?"

Everyone had thought about it. No one had actually done anything.

Lee, thinking out loud, said, "Dr. Byrd is going to expect us to put something in the mail every Friday. That only gives us two days this week. We need to send in something even if we change our minds later."

Winnie Clifton added, "I guess we should start at the beginning."

"It's a very good place to start," Vera sang.

"When you read you begin with A-B-C," Sister joined in, drawing on her Broadway class.

Before I knew what had happened, the entire group and I were dancing around the big house singing "Do-Re-Me" with Vera pointing out who should sing which note. We'd just finished; everyone busted out laughing when Vera launched into, "The hills are alive . . ."

"That's enough, Maria. Seriously, where are we going to start?" Winnie was focused.

"Let's start off easy with how Rowja got its name."

"Oh, that's just ducky," Susie B. snorted.

"You'll be fine. Let's everybody tell what we know about the story. Speedy, you take notes. Dr. Byrd won't be expecting much since we're just getting started, and it's a short week," Sister was on a roll.

"Then we can reorganize it, and clean it up tomorrow. Friday morning, we can type it up, proofread, make corrections, and get it in the mail by Friday afternoon."

"Winnie, you just beat all."

"Oh, that'll be good," said Sister, "We can go to the fish fry at MiMi's with a clear conscience."

"What's a fish fry?" Merril asked.

"You'll just have to find out for yourself. Let's get started. Speedy, try to keep up."

Here's what I wrote.

How Rowja Got Its Name

Our people come from Rowja, Texas. Nobody knows where that is. Even if they think they know, they don't. Folks seem convinced that it's somewhere down by the border with Mexico. Rowja is in deep East Texas, the Piney Woods. The best way to find it is to look at a map of the Great State of Texas. Now, go to the eastern border. It goes straight for a while and then commences to squiggling. Just keep looking around, and if the map has small enough towns, you'll find Rowja.

Pronouncing Rowja can also be a problem. Folks don't have too much trouble with the "row" part. But the "ja" part gives them fits. My granddaddy tells people that it's easy enough—"Row" like your boat and "ha" like Bob Wills would say after "ah." If people don't know who Bob Wills is, Granddaddy sighs, calls them poorly educated and puts in his tape of San Antonio Rose.

A whole lot of this part of Texas was covered up by the ocean, so the soil in parts of the area is real sandy and makes for growing some fine watermelons. Just about where we are the ocean quit, and the land took over. At some of the places kind of in between, you can burrow into the sides of gulleys and find shark teeth and other sorts of fossils. Going to dig for shark teeth is one of our field trip options. About the only other option is to go to the chicken processing plant. Shark teeth were more fun even if you do get stuck by blackberry vines or bit by chiggers. Anyhow, Rowja is about where the ocean played out completely and has red clay dirt that's nearly about impossible to dig a post hole in.

That's the geography part. The history part comes in when the Spanish came through looking for gold or trying to save the Indians from the eternal fires depending on who was teaching that year. They must have been trying to dig a post hole or something because there are records marking this area as "roja," or red, due to the red dirt. They're right about it. The dirt is red, the creeks run red, and the dust blows red. Even worse, it won't come out of your clothes so a whole lot of us walk around with red knees and elbows. If you were looking for a place to call red dirt, this would be a good one.

Sooner or later, settlers started crossing over from America. There's a lot of reasons why they came over, but it didn't have anything to do with saving the Indians and really are stories for another time. The Spanish were long gone—no gold.

When they stopped and asked the people who lived here what this place was called, they got the answer Roja. Now the Americans didn't know anything about speaking Spanish and decided that the natives couldn't speak good English and were trying to say Row Hard like you'd have to row hard to make it up the river to get here. Rowing up the Sabine River would be nigh onto impossible, but that's what they decided. When it came time to write it down, some sort of big fight happened about how to spell it. The natives wanted Roja, the Americans wanted Rowhard. Before there was any killing a great figure in the early history of East Texas Miz Beatrice Beall Burton, Susie's B's ancestor, stepped forward and proposed a compromise combining the two. "Row" for the Americans and "ja" for the natives. "Row" came first and was capitalized because it was the American part and Miz Burton was American. And that's how Rowja got its name.

Fish Fry

Going to a fish fry out at Aunt MiMi's house was always an experience, especially if Aunt Jewel felt so inclined to make the table talk. Sister, her friends, and I all piled in to the Do-doe. The Do-doe was an old Dodge van that had been sent to pasture as a farm truck after many years of service as the McRiley's delivery van. It still had the light-up delivery sign on top, a mortar and pestle with McRiley's M & M so you'd know who it was that was pulling up to your house.

The Do-doe was so named because somebody at the Dodge plant messed up. Instead of the chrome letters on the front of the van reading D O D G E, ours read D O D O E. The crazy thing was that we'd had it seven or eight years before Sister looked down and said "Had y'all noticed that this van says Do-doe?"

By now, it rode about like you'd expect a Do-doe to ride. The springs in the seats were a little sprung, it squeaked and squawked like a clarinet with a bad reed, and it refused to go more than about forty miles an hour. But it held everybody, and you could get to MiMi's using dirt roads, so it was perfect for the trip over. Sister even planned to light up the McRiley's M & M sign on the way home after it got dark.

The fish fry was in full swing when we got there. MiMi had a nice, large house on the banks of Lake Burton. The house used to be way down the hill, but when they decided to dam up the river, MiMi's land was going to be flooded. The state paid her for her land and picked up her house and hauled it to a hilltop that was now lakefront property.

Doc and MiMi were out in the yard manning the fish fryer and the chicken fryer respectively. Everybody had brought something either already cooked or ready to drop in one of the fryers scattered about the yard. Orange extension cords were draped through the pines like grapevines. The food was displayed on three tables that had been constructed by putting old doors on top of sawhorses. All in all, it was quite an assortment–corn on the cob, turnip greens, pink-eyed purple hulls, a half dozen or so congealed salads, hush puppies, fried okra, nickel pickles, tater tots, and enough cakes, watermelons, homemade ice cream, cobblers, and pies for a county fair. To drink, we had iced tea, Co-Colas, Falstaff beer, red Kool-Aid, milk, and lake-tasting water. Long Sunday School tables and folding chairs were scattered between the house and the lake, so that people could sit and eat and fellowship. The people present ranged in age from six months to ninety-four.

Of course, my sister's friends were the center of that particular universe. My relatives were bombarding them with questions—some that made sense, others that did not. My particular favorite was my cousin who asked Merril if they still had snow on the ground. He seemed convinced that East Aurora, New York, was one county over from Santa's workshop.

On top of that, the various aunts were insisting that Sister's friends "have just a bite" of ever type of food possible. It was especially troublesome because the friends didn't know how to properly refuse something. Even if you didn't want a particular dish because you just didn't want it you still had to provide an appropriate compliment—"No ma'am. I just couldn't. It surely does look mighty pretty though," or "No ma'am. I wish I'd known about it before I filled up on those good peas you made." Otherwise, folks just think you're showing good manners by carrying through with the three-refusal ritual. If you've had a lot to eat or if your plate is piled sky-high, you should refuse more food three times before taking any. It goes something like this:

"Can I offer you a slice of pie?"

"No, thank you."

"Are you sure? It's mighty tasty."

"Oh no, I couldn't."

"It was my Grandmama's recipe."

"Really, I'm stuffed." By not giving a specific reason why you're stuffed, you keep the ritual going.

"I made it just for you, and I'll be so disappointed if you don't eat even just a little."

"Well, maybe just a sliver."

Vera and Merril had no idea about this tradition. They'd refuse something three times and then continue to refuse. They couldn't understand why three, or really even two no thank yous were insufficient, and the family members couldn't understand how many times or ways it was necessary to ask.

After everyone had eaten to complete discomfort, folks began splitting into groups of interest. Some went down to the lake to swim. Others went out in the Jon boats to do a little fishing. One group went out on the front porch to sit on some rickety old chairs, the swing, or an old church pew MiMi had seen floating in the lake after it was flooded. She'd gone out in her pontoon boat, hooked it with the handle of her umbrella, tied it to the boat, and brought it to shore. She got a couple of her grandkids to drag it to the front porch. Once it dried out, she painted it school bus yellow because that was the color they had at the Surplus Salvage store. It was her pride and joy. The front porch group would play guitars and sing whatever came to mind. "On the Wings of a Snow White Dove" could be followed by "Your Cheatin' Heart" or the one that goes "A Buzzard Took a Monkey for a Ride in the Air."

Doc and his cronies set up a couple of card tables in the parlor for 42 games. 42 is an East Texas domino game with rules that change according to family and location. It's kind of confusing. If you've ever played Spades, it's sort of like that except with dominoes and math.

Sister and her friends and I went to the dining room with Me-Mama, MiMi, and Aunt Jewel because Aunt Jewel was of a mind to have a table talking. When we sat down at the big round table, Aunt Jewel said, "We need at least two more people. The spirits need more energy. Go out to the porch and get a couple of the bad singers. If we're going to listen to all that caterwauling, it may as well be in key."

I was dispatched to collect a couple of my cousins. I wound up with three because they were excited about the table talking.

Table Talking

You might not know what a table talking is. It's what fancy folks call a séance. Table talking in my family is not nearly as formal as the séances on TV or at the movies. First off, the lights are on, and you don't have to close your eyes. Second off, we don't use candles. We've had enough people watch their heart pine houses burn up that candles aren't very popular. Third off, it doesn't need to be quiet. Like tonight, there's generally a rollicking 42 game going on in the next room. I've never heard tell of a quiet 42 game. There's yelling laughter, whooping, cussing, and general carrying on. Also, the caterwaulers were still out on the front porch.

Even with all that, Aunt Jewel was able to contact the other side with a good deal of regularity. One of my personal favorites was when the spirits revealed the name of Sister's 10th grade crush.

Sister was about to explain table talking to her pals when much to everyone's surprise Merril seemed peculiarly well-informed on the subject due to her hometown being near to a place called Lilly Dale. Lilly Dale must be spooky central, because spiritualists and mediums come from all over the place to hold Tarot and palm readings, have séances, and generally confer with the dearly departed. They even have some kind of sacred stump where they hold mass readings. Three or four mediums will take turns finding people in the audience who have relatives looking to send them a message. Merril allowed as to how it was good fun. She'd been a few times with friends, but no one from the other side seemed to want to talk to her.

Lee, Susie B. and Vera were not as well informed on the subject, so Sister gave them a quick lesson on what was going on. Aunt Jewel normally would cover the rules, but she was already in her chair humming with her eyes closed. Winnie, of course, had attended various talking ceremonies through the years, including the revelation of the crush even though it wasn't a revelation to her.

"Just pull up and put your hands on the table," said Sister. "Kind of spread out your fingers. Let your thumbs touch each other and your pinky fingers touch the pinkies of your neighbors. So Susie B., your pinkies need to be touching Winnie's and Lee's. Try your best not to break the circle."

"What if I get freaked out?" Lee asked.

"Don't. The spirits can only answer yes or no questions. If you want to know a name or something, you have to spell out letters until the table tells you you've got it."

I chimed in. "Like if you have a crush on a boy, and his name is Greg, then you'd have to spell, A-B-C-D-E-F-G, and then the table will say 'yes.' Then you start on the second letter until you finally figure out his name, and then . . ."

"That's good enough." Sister did not want to go through being teased about Greg Austin, Tommy Austin's older brother.

"How do you know if the answer is yes or no?"

"Whoever we get will knock on the table once for yes and twice for no. It's a general rule in the spirit world."

Lee asked quietly, "How do we know it's not somebody at the table who's doing the rapping?"

"We have our eyes open and everybody's hands are touching."

"Couldn't somebody be kicking under the middle of the table?"

I noticed that Aunt Jewel had cracked her right eye open just enough to send Lee an evil squint.

"I don't know how. Nobody around here is enough of a contortionist that they could manage to kick the table without showing the effort. And, this table is pretty high. You'd need to be a Rangerette or Apache Bell to pull that off."

Aunt Jewel closed her eye and smiled a little.

"Rangerettes and Apache Bells?" Merril's knowledge of the supernatural did not extend to this level.

"Those are dance squads for a couple of the junior colleges around here. They do routines like The Rockettes. I think you can even major in Rockette-ery at those schools."

Before matters got any more confusing, Aunt Jewel pronounced, "I believe I'm ready . . . Are the spirits present?"

No one breathed. Nothing happened.

"Are the spirits present?" Aunt Jewel asked a little louder.

Still nothing.

Apparently the spirits were operating under the rule of threes that night because right after Aunt Jewel called out the third time, "Are the spirits present?" sure as shooting, right in the middle of the table there was a muffled sounding thump that vibrated through our fingers.

"I heard something," Susie B. gasped.

"Heard it? I felt it." Vera exclaimed in her best Tallulah Bankhead.

"Do you think it was really a spirit?" Lee asked.

At that, the table reared up on two legs and slammed down hard.

"Don't break the circle," Sister, Aunt Jewel, and Merril hollered. Then they all looked at one another and smiled as though they knew something we didn't.

"Spirit, are you here tonight with a particular message?"

A good solid thwack sounded in the middle of the table.

"Can we know your first name?"

YES.

"Tell us when we get to the first letter–A-B-C-D-E-F-G-H-I-J-K-L"

"Too bad it's not Ada," one of the cousins whispered, earning a glare from Aunt Jewel.

"M-N-O-P-Q-R-S-T"

YES

"The first letter is T?"

YES.

"The second letter–A-B-C-D-E-F-G-H-I-J-K-L-M-N-O"

YES.

"The third letter, is it–A-B-C-D-E-F-G-H-I-J-K-L-M"

YES.

At this point, I began to feel a little creeped out myself and kind of sick to my stomach. I was hoping it was too much lemon pie, but I looked around and saw the same sort of queasy look on Sister's face. She asked what I was thinking. "Are you Tommy Austin?"

NO. The table thumped twice.

I took a deep breath and put my head down on the table because I was feeling a little faintified. I don't know why the thought of having Tommy Austin show up bothered me so much. It just did.

"Is your name Tom?" Aunt Jewel carried on.

YES

"Will you tell us your last name?"

Nothing. We were all concentrating trying to hear. The singers and domino players might as well have been in the next county for all the attention we were paying them.

"Can we know your last name?"

Still nothing.

"Spirit, are you there?"

YES.

"All right, we'll go ahead on, then."

"Do you have a message for anyone in particular?"

YES.

"That's fine, Tom. I'll go around the table and you let me know when I get there. Do you have a message for me?"

NO.

"Do you have a message for Naomi?"

NO.

"Do you have a message for Sister?"

YES.

I saw my sister's shoulders slump. I just knew she was dreading an updated Greg Austin message.

"Good. Let's try to find out what the message is."

All of a sudden it was like the table got mad. It took to bucking and dancing all over the place.

Everybody except Aunt Jewel looked surprised and a little scared but managed to hold on while Aunt Jewel shouted, "Is the message for others as well?"

YES. The table banged extra loud and then settled back down.

"Is it for Winnie?"

YES.

"Is that all?" Aunt Jewel asked, trying to avoid another tantrum.

NO.

"Is it for Susie B.?"

YES.

My sister looked relieved. Winnie and Susie B. looked positively slack-jawed, soon to be joined by . . .

"Is it for Lee Harris?"

YES.

"Is it for, honey, I'm sorry, I've done misplaced your name."

"Vera," she said softly with a complete absence of drama.

YES.

"Is it for Merle?"

"Merril," Sister whispered.

YES.

"Is it for Esther?" That was Me-Mama.

NO

"Is it for Speedy?"

NO

I admit to feeling relieved when I guess Tom changed his mind and the table banged down—YES.

"Let's give it another go to be sure. Is the message for Speedy, too?"

YES

Before Aunt Jewel could move on, the table took to dancing again.

"Is that everybody, Tom?"

YES.

The cousins seemed disappointed. Sister and her friends all looked a tad puny. I guess I did, too.

"Well, Tom, let's see what you want to tell the college girls and Speedy," Aunt Jewel commenced to spelling.

You know how it works now, so I won't go through all the spelling we did with Tom. I'll just tell you what Aunt Jewel asked and what Tom answered.

"Tom, what is your message?"

F-I-N-D M-E

"Are you lost?"

YES.

"Are your folks looking for you?"

NO

"Why not?"

No answer.

"Was anybody ever looking for you?"

YES

"If they find you, do you want anything else?"

K-N-O-W M-E

"It would help if we knew his last name," Winnie pointed out.

"Tom, will you tell us your last name?"

Still nothing.

"Tom, do you want them to know what happened to you?"

YES

"Would you like them to find out how you died?"

Nothing.

"Do you think he knows he's dead?" Winnie ventured. All in all, it was a reasonable question.

YES—followed by more of the impatient dancing.

Sister pondered, "I wonder if he died alone and they never found his body and that's why he wants us to find him. Aunt Jewel, could you please ask him?"

"Tom, did you die alone?"

NO

"Did you get buried around here somewhere?"

YES

"Ooh, see if he's under the lake like in that movie," a cousin blurted out.

Aunt Jewel sighed, but asked anyway, "Tom, are you under the lake?"

NO

Sister and her friends seemed relieved that we weren't going to go diving in Lake Burton looking for a cemetery.

"Tom, does your grave have a marker?"

YES

"If we knew when he died it would at least help us narrow down the search," Susie B. pointed out.

"Well, ask him."

At this time, no one seemed to find it the least bit peculiar that the Summester project was expanding to include a search for the grave of somebody named Tom who was first introduced to us through a bouncing table.

MiMi sighed. "Oh mercy, Susie B., about when did your people get here? I don't 'spect there were any Indians or Mexicans named Tom."

"Spaniards," Me-Mama corrected.

"Them neither."

Aunt Jewel looked annoyed, but said, "Susie B., we just need a general starting point."

"It was not long after the War of 1812."

"All right, just to be safe. Did you die in the 1700s?"

"NO"

"Did you die in the 1800s?"

NO

"The 1900s?"

YES

"Here we go 1-2-3-4-5-6-7-8-9-10-11-12-13-14-15-16"

YES

"1916?"

YES

"Aunt Jewel, maybe we should find out how he died. You know sometimes gravestones back then had a poem or some kind of sentiment that would be a clue."

"Tom, how did you die?"

We were all holding our breath as the table banged out M-U-R-

All of a sudden, there was a huge crash, a great commotion, lots of non-Biblical cussing, and howls of laughter coming from the 42 room.

Doc and Uncle Parker came walking in. Doc was looking particularly pleased and Uncle Parker looked ready to strangulate Doc. "Y'all about through? I just set Parker on him going low with the ace-deuce. He threw it out the window and knocked the table over. I 'spect it'll be morning afore we can find it."

"Doc, I swear, you just draw trouble," MiMi said.

I wasn't sure if she was talking about Uncle Parker going set on a domino that should have just sailed through, Uncle Parker's reaction, or the silent table when Aunt Jewel asked, quietly, "Tom are you there?" He was not.

The party broke up soon after with the 42 players hoorah-ing Parker, the singers coming to the end of their repertoire, and the table talkers looking around trying to decide where they'd all been for the last hour or so.

Everybody began loading into their cars and trucks. I could hear snatches of pleasantries.

"Thanks for having us Aunt MiMi."

"We'll do it again before the summer gets away."

"Your house is lovely."

"Say 'hello' to your Mama and 'em for me."

"See you Thursday."

"It was so nice to get to know you."

"Take some of this casserole."

"It was all mighty fine."

"Doc, put down that stick. I swear. Nobody thinks it's a snake."

Me-Mama started in with what, for her, was a short lecture: "It was so good to meet you girls. Come back anytime. Let us know if we can help with your school work. Holler if you need anything. Do we need to follow you to the big house? No? Well, then, Sister call your daddy when you get there. I'll call him and tell him to be expecting your call. Blink the porch light, so Peter will know it's you."

We finally extracted ourselves and our Cool Whip containers full of leftovers, started up the Do-doe, and headed down the road.

Merril asked what we'd all been wondering: "Who do you think murdered Tom?"

The mood was so somber Sister didn't even light up the McRiley's sign on the way back.

Change of Plans

It was a strange night at the Big House. The usual practice was for everyone to sit around the dining room table or out on the front porch talking about everything and nothing all at once. The night after the table talking everybody just got ready for bed and retired for the evening.

The next morning, we were sitting around breakfast, still quiet, when Merril asked, "Do you think we ought to tell Dr. Byrd about this?" She had obviously been pondering the question overnight.

"I don't know," Winnie allowed. "It depends on whether this is going to be what we're working on. You have to admit we've lacked focus."

Lee Harris spoke up, "Are y'all really thinking about basing our entire Summester project on a table bounding around a room?"

Everyone else looked at one another, balancing their previous night's certainty with their morning reality.

"Yes," Sister hazarded.

"I can't see why not," Merril chimed in.

"Well, Miss Lilly Dale, maybe your people don't think communing with the dead is anything out-of-the-ordinary, but come on y'all, this is just crazy. Besides, what sort of grade are we going to get chasing a ghost?"

"Lee doesn't mean to be insulting, Merril," Susie B. said addressing the look on Merril's face.

"Oh, I don't know. We could use the table talking as our theme and base our project on trying to solve the mystery. It's like Winnie said, it gives our project focus," Sister said.

"Right." Vera was getting fired up, "We could look for Tom—go through cemeteries, courthouse records, and newspapers. We could write up the search, and then when we find him we could work on figuring out how he was killed and who killed him."

"When we find him?" Lee was not happy. I guess having crazy Bertie in your family might make you leery of anything that might seem unconventional.

"I don't know, Lee. It might be kind of fun. It's a whole lot better than just doing a straight up chronology of the county." Susie B. was showing some enthusiasm.

Winnie laughed, "In 1883, this happened. In 1884, that happened. In 1885, something happened, but no one remembers what it was. In 1886, nothing happened."

"I'm bored to my very toes thinking about it," Vera yawned.

"But y'all, think about it. A séance? Melanie's aunt was bouncing the table around. I don't know how she was doing it. Some of those cousins she had you bring in were probably helping." Lee was speaking faster and faster.

"I wouldn't mention that around her. There's talk that she can conjure," Sister warned with a Doc-like twinkle in her eye.

"Lee, it just doesn't matter," Winnie plowed ahead. "Whether Tom is out there we can use our experience last night as a jumping off point. Even if there's no Tom, we have a point of reference. The search becomes the story. We'll write about all the characters and culture we encounter as we explore."

"And, that, my friends, is why Winnie is at the top of the class," Susie B. pointed out.

"But it can't be real. People will think we are crazy. It's just not true. We'd be chasing a phantom." Lee was getting more frantic.

"Oh, crazier things than this have happened around here," Winnie responded, "And again, it doesn't matter. The chase is what's important, not the phantom. You're right. Our imaginations ran off the road last night. We're not looking for Tom. We're using Tom as a clarifying device. So what if Tom doesn't exist?"

"But what if he did?" Merril asked.

"Then we have an even cooler project," Sister claimed.

Everyone around the table was nodding, talking, and laughing at the prospect of solving a murder from 1916, except for Lee who looked like she was about to tune up and cry.

"I swear, Lee. You'd think you had been the one who murdered Tom," Vera teased.

"Vera, hush." Susie B., the most kind hearted of the bunch, tried to help. "Nobody's going to think we're crazy. We'll put everything in context."

"Right," Winnie added. "The table talking can be an example of local folklore and culture, and then we can write the paper using all these different types of resources–newspapers, maps, records, interviews. It's the kind of thing that will set our project apart."

Lee looked a little less panic-stricken. She seemed to be able tell by looking at the others that they were excited about using the search for Tom as the basis for their project. She made one last attempt to squelch the idea. "I just don't know what Dr. Byrd is going to think about this."

"Oh, she'll love it," Vera proclaimed.

"Vera, you can't know that."

The whole bunch began talking at once about what they thought Dr. Byrd would think. Vera even allowed to how they might want to get aunt Jewel to consult the spirits regarding the issue.

After several minutes of following this debate, I asked what I thought was the obvious question. "Why don't you ask her?"

Sister about fell out laughing, "Speedy, that's a most practical suggestion. I'll go call Me-Mama to see if it's okay to make a long distance call. I don't think Dr. Byrd would be interested in reversing the charges."

"Before we call, we should also see if she's interested in getting a call on the weekend."

Winnie went to her room and came back with a folder of papers. "She has a number on the syllabus for nights and weekends. She just asks that we don't call before ten in the morning or after seven at night and to not get put out if she doesn't answer the phone."

"Well, it's 10:15 right now, so I'm going to go call Me-Mama." Sister was gone a couple of minutes and returned, saying, "She'd gone to the store, so I talked to Doc. He's all in favor of 'keeping the flame of education burning for all to admire'. He also wants to know what happened to Tom. He wants us to do this in a call lasting less than five minutes."

"You people are all insane," Lee said.

"Do we agree that Winnie makes the call?"

General agreement rang from around the table, except for Lee. I had the feeling that Lee wanted to call Dr. Byrd to convince her that this was one of the most dim-witted ideas ever to be proposed. Either that or she was going to ask if she could be assigned to another group.

Winnie wrote out a few notes to use as a script, excused herself, and went to the telephone table in the front room. We listened, but couldn't make out the conversation.

Winnie obeyed Granddaddy's orders, and when she came back less than five minutes later, she gave away nothing until she grinned and said, "Dr. Byrd is intrigued. She thinks it's about the 'funnest,' yes, she said funnest Summester project she's heard about. She said to go for it and keep her updated."

Everybody cheered and hoorah-ed except for Lee, who closed her eyes, looked up at the ceiling, and took in a deep breath.

Vera ran to the back door, slung it open and hollered, "Hold on Tom. We'll find you."

Winnie's Been Busy

After talking to Dr. Byrd everyone headed their own way to visit with their families in the area. Vera went out to the Millers' and Winnie Clifton just stayed at our house where she already had a room. It was generally agreed upon that Merril would go from house to house depending on the weekend. This particular weekend she was staying with Lee at her Uncle Stuart's and Aunt Rachel's house. Uncle Stuart was one of Bertie and Lee's granddaddy's brothers, so Merril got a good solid warning about Bertie. Everyone was to meet back up at the Big House on Sunday night.

This is probably as good a time as any to tell you more about Lee's Rayburn County relatives. Lee's great-great grandfather, Sam Houston Harris, was killed in the cornfield along with most of the other Texans in General Hood's regiment at the Battle of Sharpsburg. You may have heard tell of this battle as the Battle of Antietam but that's an argument for another day. He left behind a widow and a young son, Travis Crockett, who made their way to Rayburn County to be near some of their kin. The son was raised with all sorts of tales about his heroic daddy and the Lost Cause.

As a result, Lee's great-granddaddy named his passel of children, all boys except for Bertie, after notables of the Confederate States—Jefferson Davis Harris, John Bell Harris, Albert Sydney Harris, Thomas Jackson Harris, James Longstreet Harris, Petey-G Beauregard Harris, Jeb Stuart Harris, and Robertie Lee Harris. We asked Granddaddy who believed he got everybody right and in more or less the correct order, but Lee was going to try to find a family Bible just to be sure.

Granddaddy also allowed as to how a lot of the family had gotten past the late unpleasantness, but that the two older brothers—Jeff and John Bell—and then their descendants had not. They lived in a bunch of double-wide trailers way out in the woods smack dab between the roads to Shreveport and Mayhaw. Lee would have rather stayed with Bertie than with any of them. The Confederate Compound, as Granddaddy called it, wasn't very far from the big house as the crow flies, but it was quite a haul if you were driving. Lee's great-uncle Tommy J. had married a girl from Reeb and settled there. John Bell, Sydney and Jimmie had died in the flu epidemic. Petey-G (Lee's granddaddy) moved away and shortened his name to Pete. Stuart and Bertie, of course, lived in Rowja.

"Y'all will not be surprised to learn that Winnie has been busy," Sister announced, once everybody had gotten back Sunday night.

Winnie *had* been busy. She had walked up to Effie Floyd after church and told her about the project—omitting the part about Tom—and asked Miz Floyd if she'd be willing to let us talk with her and maybe go through some of her newspapers. Miz Floyd was always eager to speak on her favorite subject—herself—so she readily agreed to have everyone over to her house on Tuesday afternoon at 3:15.

Tuesday was a good day because the *Trumpet Stampede* came out twice a week, Wednesday and Sunday. Those were the best days for reporting on local junior high and high school games during the school year. Miz Floyd wrote her column on Mondays—that being the day most convenient for reporting on scoops obtained at church—and Thursdays—that being a good day to report on stories collected at the beauty parlor, grocery store, and prayer meeting. She had her hair done on Tuesday morning with a touch-up on Friday morning. Her weekly grocery run took place on Wednesday. She would collect the fliers from the *Trumpet Stampede* and creep her way from store to store to take advantage of the weekly specials. Every afternoon until 3:00 was reserved for watching her stories.

Miz Floyd also told Winnie that she would get her a key to the archives—the shed that held the newspapers—but that the girls were only to use it if they promised to lock up.

I went to ball practice on Monday while the Altheans worked on questions to ask Effie Floyd. We had a game that night with Mayhaw. Pretty much every little town in Rayburn County had a team. Rowja had enough players to make up three teams. Burtonville had two. Every team played each other at least once in the summer. There weren't many league rules. You had to be in school, but it didn't matter how old or young you were or if you were a girl until toward the end of the year when the grown-ups got together to pick all-county teams. These teams were divided into age groups, and girls couldn't play. Rayburn County sent these all-county teams out to compete in state-wide competition because those folks were way more particular. Most of us thought winning the county was more impressive because the best people got to play no matter what.

Sister was going to play center field because we still hadn't replaced Tommy Austin, but she didn't have to practice because she was Sister. Just so you won't be in suspense, I'll let you know that WE WON! The Altheans all came as a cheering section. Vera kept encouraging us to smite them. We won when Jodell drove in the winning run—me!—with a triple or a single with a couple of errors depending on how you saw it. The ball originally went into left field, but by the time the Mayhaw players threw it around the countryside, Jodell was standing on third. I started off on first base because I had walked and just kept running as hard as I could. I kept going as long as I was hearing Sister yell "Run Speedy, run like the wind." Jodell later told us she considered running home just to see where they'd throw it next, but thought better of it when she figured out she might beat me to the plate.

After the game, both teams gathered for watermelon and ice cream from McRiley's. The world famous Rowja watermelons weren't full ripe yet, so we had some that had been trucked up from the Valley. Everybody had a good time when we played Mayhaw. Most of the Mayhaw team was kin to me in one way or another. I told you earlier that my Daddy's people came from Mayhaw or the suburbs of Mayhaw. Me-Mama had ten brothers and sisters and Granddaddy had eleven brothers and sisters, so a whole slew of folks from Mayhaw were either kin or kin-in-law. The family lines crossed and uncrossed so many times that it could be hard to tell who was kin and who wasn't. Daddy said we didn't have a family tree so much as a briar patch.

Anyhow, folks from Rowja and folks from Mayhaw generally got along just dandy. The story would be different when we played the hooligans–Me-Mama's word–from Reeb, or even worse, the team from Hannibal.

The next morning we were still celebrating what Vera called the glorious victory as we prepared to head to town. We were going to have dinner at Me-Mama's and Granddaddy's house before heading to Effie Floyd's.

Winnie spent most of the morning making the others figure out questions: the questions that they had to ask, the questions they wanted to ask, and the extra questions in the unlikely chance that Miz Floyd wasn't in the mood to talk. She also made sure that the tape recorder and a spare were both working and inventoried the batteries and cassette tapes to make sure that they had enough. She also directed everybody to carry notebooks, paper, and pens.

"Before we go, we need to attend to a little business," Winnie continued. "Merril, we need to try to establish more specifically how you might be connected to Rowja. Can you think of anyone who might be able to fill in any sort of detail?"

Sister jumped in. "The postcard isn't enough?"

"I just think the project will be better received if we have something more definitive. If there's nothing to add, we'll go with the postcard, but it can't hurt to show we've made an effort."

No one was going to question Winnie's assessment of what would make the paper "better received."

"My grandmother might remember something, but she's in a retirement home and doesn't always have a good grasp of . . ." Merril's voice dropped away.

Vera, trying to be helpful, interjected, "If she's anything like my Aunt Sally, she'll remember 1920 better than what she had for breakfast."

"Vera, that's just tacky," said Susie B.

"Tacky maybe, but true. It's worth a try."

"I could write my mother and ask her to ask my grandmother what she remembers," ventured Merril.

"Well, get crackin'," Winnie ordered.

"Now?"

"Why not? They aren't expecting us for dinner for over an hour. Write her a line or two, and we can drop it off at the post office on the way to Effie Floyd's. Who knows how long it will take it to get there and get an answer back?"

"Maybe it will be there by Saturday delivery. My parents visit Grandmother on Sundays."

"Why not just call her?"

"I'd hate to reverse the charges twice in one week. I'll talk to her Saturday as usual. If she hasn't gotten the letter by then, I can fill her in. She won't go visit Grandmother until Sunday regardless." Merril headed to the desk in her room to write the note. She called back over her shoulder, "I will not be mentioning Tom." She winked as she turned the corner.

"Good plan. The fewer who know about that, the better," Lee Harris called back. "They'd probably make you room with your grandmother after they came down here and snatched you up."

"Be snappy about it," Sister hollered. "We need to leave in thirty minutes or else Doc will turn into Grumpy." That was a long-time family joke.

Merril completed her homework in good order, and we all piled into the Do-Doe. We took it even though we would be traveling on a paved road with a speed limit that exceeded the Do-Doe's capabilities. It was all right because first, it would be broad daylight the entire time we'd be out. Second, everybody in the county knew the Do-Doe and understood that was as fast as it would go and that if they wanted to go faster, they could durn sure go around. Finally, we were expected to be at Granddaddy's and Me-Mama's house by a certain time. If we were running real late, they'd know to come look for us on the side of the road.

As we were driving to Rowja, Sister said matter-of-factly, "I need to warn you about eating at Me-Mama's house."

Dinner at Doc's and Me-Mama's

I started to snicker. Winnie giggled.

"Why? What's the matter with it?"

"Nothing, it's good. It's just that her meals are color-coded."

Winnie snorted.

"Color-coded?!" Vera exclaimed.

"Yes, there are a couple of brown meals, a dark-brown and a light brown and a kind of creamy-yellow meal. Every now and then she crosses us up, but those are the main ones. Oh, and please understand that the term 'vegetable' is broadly defined."

"Should we be worried?"

"Heavens, no." Winnie was still chuckling.

"My favorite is the light brown meal," Sister began.

"Mine's the creamy yellow," I jumped in.

"The light brown meal—fried chicken, purple hull peas, homemade rolls, cornbread . . . yes, rolls *and* cornbread, tater tots and some sort of fried pie for dessert—peach, apple, or pear. The creamy-yellow meal is chicken and dumplings, Texas toast . . ."

"What's Texas toast?" Merril had reached her limit.

"It's thick bread that's been slathered in butter and toasted," Winnie offered.

Sister picked back up, "Chicken and dumplings, Texas toast, cream peas, corn-on-the-cob, and favorite pie."

"At the risk of sounding like a broken record, what's favorite pie?" Vera chimed in.

I was puzzled because I'd never really thought about it. Sister did the best she could, "I'm not sure. It's Me-Mama's Mama's recipe and Me-Mama's sister Julia's favorite. When you ask Me-Mama how to make it she just declares that we don't need to worry about it. She'll just make us one. Anyway, the dark brown meal is fried hamburger steak. Me-Mama puts flour in the patties before she fries them, so they'll hold the grease and be juicy. Plus macaroni and cheese . . ."

"Shouldn't macaroni and cheese be in the yellowish meal?"

"Clearly, you have not seen the cheese," Winnie howled.

"Ahem. Macaroni and cheese, green beans or turnip greens, sometimes both . . ."

"How are green beans and turnip greens brown? They have green right there in their names?" said Vera.

"We do not serve our beans or greens rare, medium rare, medium or even medium well. Like our macaroni and cheese, our beans and greens are served well done, very well done. Trust me. They are dark brown verging on black. And so again I proceed. Hamburger steak, macaroni and cheese, turnip greens or green beans or both, cornbread . . ."

"You said cornbread was part of the light brown meal." Vera had been paying attention.

"Turn it over. The bottom is dark brown. And we try again. Hamburger steak, macaroni and cheese, turnip greens or green beans or both, cornbread, and pecan pie."

"Are you honestly telling us those three meals are the only ones you ever eat?"

"No, on Sundays we often have the dark brown meal with roast instead of hamburger steak, along with some extra sides. Sometimes we'll have ham or chicken salad sandwiches, and there's almost always homemade pickles and chili sauce to bring a little spirit of Christmas to the table. But I'd say those three are our most likely candidates."

"They're all real good, and Me-Mama likes to point out that she hasn't killed anyone yet," I noted.

"So very true. Now, we're about here, so everyone maintain your composure. Winnie, I'm afraid you may have to claim an allergy attack or something. Your eyes are watery, and your face is sort of red and squonched up."

"Will do."

We parked the Do-Doe behind Granddaddy's farm truck. We'd probably be taking Me-Mama's Imperial to Effie Floyd's and either Mama's or Daddy's car depending on who drove to work that day. The plates, tea, silverware, napkins, salt and pepper, pickles, and chili sauce were on the table. Me-Mama, Granddaddy, and MiMi were watching the end of one of their stories. They'd set the table during the commercials.

"Y'all hush up. I want to see what that hussy is going to do," MiMi cautioned.

"You can see it tomorrow when they show it thirty-four more times. Let's eat."

"Doc, now you just–oooohhhh, what did I tell you? Looky what that back-stabbin' no good–well, I suwannee—that ain't right—they need to go ahead and show us what's behind that door," MiMi complained as the theme music played.

"They'll show you in a week or two. Let's eat."

Me-Mama turned away from the squabbling and asked, "Winnie, are you feeling all right?"

"Yes ma'am. I just seem to have the sinus this morning."

MiMi jumped in, "I saw the highway department mowing this morning. I imagine that was it."

"Yes ma'am."

We began negotiating who would sit where when Me-Mama instructed, "Doc, just hold on a minute before you say the blessing. I need to get them rolls out of the oven."

"Just sit down. I'll say the blessing, and then you can get the rolls."

"All right, but don't be complaining to me if the rolls are burned."

He began by bellowing, "DEAR LORD." I'm guessing that eyes popped open around the table. I kept mine closed, so I can't be for certain. Several years back, MiMi observed that she couldn't hear the blessing. Granddaddy allowed as to how he wasn't praying to her. Since then every so often he would begin the blessing by addressing "the balcony." This was one of those times. He then talked really fast "Thank-you-for-these-and-all-our-many-blessings. Esther-get-the-rolls. Amen."

"Doc, that ole bad man's gonna get you."

Me-Mama and MiMi went in the kitchen and brought back platters and bowls full of food.

It was the light brown meal, and it was delicious.

Effie Floyd

After dinner, everybody pitched in to clean up the table, wash and dry, and put away the dishes. We didn't have to put up a lot of leftovers, which led Doc to proclaim that the locusts were bad this year. We would work really hard mostly during the commercials of the twelve o'clock news on Channel 12 out of Shreveport. When a story would start, MiMi would shush everybody until it was determined if the story was of the least concern to us. If it was a national story we'd just keep at it because nothing was official until Walter Cronkite talked about it.

Silence was strictly enforced during the weather. The weatherman, Al Bolton, was judged to have a direct line to the Almighty where that was concerned. We mostly watched Channel 12 all day. I'm not sure if it was because it was the best station or if it just came in the best. The next best was Channel 3, Shreveport's ABC station. Channel 6, the NBC station, came in good sometimes, but not so good others. It didn't come in good at all in the summer. MiMi thought it had something to do with the moon landing.

We had to work fast because Doc, MiMi, and Me-Mama had to be in their chairs before the world started turning. *As the World Turns* and the *Guiding Light* were not to be missed except for the direst of emergencies.

One time a while back, Daddy had shown up for dinner right after the story was over. Daddy always showed up at strange times depending on how busy the store was. He walked in on Me-Mama and several of his aunts sitting around sobbing. This was back when Granddaddy was still at McRiley's, so he wasn't there.

"Mama, what's happened?"

"Oh honey, it's the most terrible thing," MiMi wailed. "There's been a horrible car wreck. Jeff is dead, and Penny's not expected to live."

Daddy allowed as to how that was terrible, made a sandwich, and went back to the store. He had no inclination to sit around a bunch of weeping women. When he got back, he mentioned the tragedy to the salesladies and several customers. They had all heard about it and agreed that it was one of the worst things that had ever happened. Everyone commiserated all afternoon, and anytime a new customer would come in the talk would start up again.

It wasn't until late that night that Mama told Daddy that Jeff and Penny were on *As the World Turns*. I think she told him when she noticed him going out to the car taking the big, black bow that went on McRiley's front door in case of a funeral. He had thought that Jeff and Penny were a couple of high school students.

Effie Floyd was as big a fan of the stories as anybody in my family. That's why our appointment wasn't until 3:15. It might have been later than that, but they'd moved the *Edge of Night* to ABC, so nobody watched it anymore. We all sat around and paid attention to the stories. They weren't hard to follow, and everybody was amused by MiMi's on-going commentary on the characters. She was particularly interested in John Dixon on the *World* and Holly and Roger on the *Light*.

Whenever there was a commercial, Me-Mama would tell us how we were going to conduct ourselves with Miz Floyd. I'm going to put all her instructions together, but they were spread out over two hours' worth of stories. Doc was to drive some of us in the Imperial. Sister would follow in Daddy's "hot rod." It was a Dodge Charger. Daddy had either driven the delivery van or ridden with Mama to get to work, so the Charger was available. Me-Mama did not want us to go through town in the Do-Doe because of what people might think, and she knew for sure that Miz Floyd did not want the Do-Doe parked out in front of her house. I took from this pronouncement that Me-Mama was none too pleased to have the Do-Doe parked in front of her house, but Sister just carried on like normal.

We were to start off by getting Miz Floyd to talk about herself before asking her about the boy in the picture or go out to the shed to go through the papers. Me-Mama recommended two topics to get her started—how she got her name and how she started working for the newspaper. She told Doc that he was to keep talking with Miz Floyd after we'd gotten the information we needed, so we'd have a chance to get out to the shed. Otherwise, she'd talk so much that it would be suppertime and we wouldn't have gotten a thing accomplished. We were to excuse ourselves, and Doc was to inquire about more episodes from Miz Floyd's life. We were always amazed at how many instructions Me-Mama could give us during a word from our sponsors.

"I have just the topics in mind. I'll start with the time Pappy O'Daniel's band came through town and he invited her to come up and dance with him and move on to the time she was Grand Marshall of the rodeo parade. I'll keep a couple in reserve, but I doubt I'll need any of them once she gets going."

Me-Mama continued giving instructions until the news break right before the last few minutes of the *Light*. MiMi spent the last commercial complaining about the woman on it who licked her tongue out before she drank her coffee. MiMi then proceeded to lick her tongue out until she was sure that we all understood why this was so terrible. We watched the last few minutes of the story, listened to a few more comments about Roger's doings on the *Light,* and were shooed out the door.

We negotiated the post office on the way to Miz Floyd's. Normally we'd avoid the post office at all costs because, during the summer, it and the drive-thru tellers at the Cattleman's Bank caused most of the traffic jams in Rowja. Other times of the year schools taking in or letting out would cause short tie-ups. We did pretty well because Sister wheeled the Charger into a space that wasn't really a space, and Winnie ran and dropped the letter in the slot inside instead of waiting in line at the mailbox. Doc positioned the Imperial so as to block any traffic that might prevent Sister from backing out. He told the girls riding with him that everyone knew the Imperial and would think it was Esther driving, and nobody messed with her. He even took off his hat and scrunched down in the seat to complete the illusion.

Miz Floyd was standing on her front porch when we arrived.

"Y'all are right on time. And Doc, I certainly wasn't expecting you. What a nice surprise," Miz Floyd fluttered.

"Now, Effie, how could I pass up the chance to spend an afternoon with you?" The buttering up had begun in earnest.

"Come on in. I've made lemonade and tea cakes." Miz Floyd showed us into the dining room. "There's room for all of us to sit at the table, and you'll be able to take notes."

We settled on seats and took a punch cup of lemonade and a tea cake. It was a good thing the cups and the cookies were small because Miz Floyd was a notoriously bad cook. Granddaddy told us that one time the fellowship committee "accidently" left her recipes out of the church cookbook. We washed down the dustiest, driest cookie any of us had ever tasted with lemonade that may have been made in the same room with the sugar bowl, but they had never met.

Doc bragged on the refreshments at length and bemoaned the fact that we'd eaten such a big dinner and that we planned to cut a watermelon later that evening. We all silently thanked him for keeping us from having to eat more.

"It's so nice to have visitors," Effie declared, "Before y'all start asking me questions, let me hear what you've been up to. I don't even know some of you. Now, I caught up with Winnie after church, and she's told me about your project, and I keep up with Melanie Catherine and Speedy through their Mama. Speedy, that surely was a terrible thing about Tommy Austin. I suppose you all are dedicating the season to him?"

Before I could allow to as how that was a right fine idea, Miz Floyd moved on. "Now dear," she said looking at Vera, "Tell me how you fit in."

Vera launched into what Sister later called a soliloquy, complete with voices and the occasional sound effect. Miz Floyd took notes. Vera ended with her plans for the future, including some of the awards she was aiming to receive. She had already won an award from the *Shreveport Journal* for her portrayal of Portia in Althea's production of the *Merchant of Venice*—an Oscar, Emmy, Tony, and perhaps a Grammy were bound to follow.

Miz Floyd took a deep breath and turned to Susie B., "And you, dear?"

"I'm Susie B. Burton, and I'm—"

Before Susie B. could get out another word, Miz Floyd was off on her own soliloquy about the grand contributions of the Burton family and how many times she had the privilege of interviewing family members and how generous they were to offer her exclusive rights to stories. This went on for quite a while because both Miz Floyd and the Burtons had a long history in the county. I was a little worried that Granddaddy was going to ask her if she had interviewed Beatrice Beall Burton her own self back in the time of the Spanish and Indians, but he just sat smiling to himself. Susie B. looked a mite embarrassed, but she was probably just as glad not to have to talk.

Next, she turned to Lee. "And tell me about yourself."

"I'm Lee Harris, Peter and Cora Harris' daughter. My great aunt and uncle still—"

"Oh, Lee Harris, bless your heart. That was just awful what happened to your cousin. Did they ever find out what caused it?"

"My cousin?" Lee was completely confused.

"Trey Harris. He was in that motorcycle accident."

"Is that who that was?" Granddaddy was pleased that at least one mystery was solved. "Well, I'll be."

"I'm sorry," Lee apologized. "There's parts of my family that I just don't know. Who was he?'

"Trey was T.J.'s son and Thomas Jackson's grandson. He was a fine fellow–not at all like some of those others—but it is a complete mystery why he had that wreck. There just didn't seem to be any rhyme or reason for it."

"That must be who Aunt Bertie was going on about. She kept talking about sin and angels and death of the sons. Uncle Stuart tried to get her on another topic, but she kept going back to it. Aunt Rachel finally said something about a cold coming on to get Bertie to go back to her garage apartment behind the house."

"That's always a wise plan." Effie turned to Merril in order to avoid continuing an awkward topic.

"I don't believe I know you, either."

"I'm Merril Reynolds from East Aurora, New York."

"You're a long way from home."

"Yes ma'am." Merril had learned to say ma'am after being faced with several episodes of temporary deafness when she had answered Me-Mama or MiMi with "yes."

Effie stared hard at Merril. "And who are your people?"

Merril seemed to have little idea how to answer that particular question. Granddaddy saved her, by saying, "We'll get around to that, Effie. Why don't you tell them a little about yourself? I bet they don't know how you got the name Effie."

"That was my daddy's doing. He was determined to have a child named after him. The first three that came along were girls. He told Mama that the next child was going to be named for him no matter what, and then here I came. Daddy's name was Franklin Ezra Jenkins, and Mama was not going to stand for a girl being named Franklina Ezrica or some other horror, but she did agree to call me by his initials, F. E., so they sounded it out and named me Effie. That broke the spell and the next two that came along were boys. Baby sister was the last of the line." She continued for a while before Granddaddy broke in.

"Was that about when you started working for the newspaper?"

"Not long after that, but very nearly then. I was going to be a schoolteacher. That was about the only job for girls back then. But Daddy started getting sick and just couldn't carry on like he had. Of course, he was planning on leaving the *Stampede* to my brothers to operate, but not a one of them showed any inclination, ambition, or talent to take over the business, much less have the gumption to run down stories. My older sisters were such featherheads that they were useless at anything other than cooking, cleaning, and raising babies. I wasn't necessarily interested in any of that."

Suddenly, I understood the problem with the teacakes.

"Daddy kept running the business end and typesetting, but I started working on stories. It was about nineteen oh five or six."

"Wow," Vera exclaimed. "Someone should do a movie."

"Yes, Nellie Bly, Ida Tarbell, and I were pioneer newspaper women, but they get all the attention." Miz Floyd ran on for a while longer. She would periodically cock her head and commence to staring at Merril, who would squirm a little. "But I still have good instincts about a story," Miz Floyd said. She closed her eyes part-ways, looked at Merril and said, "And I suspect you have a good one. Do you have any people in Rowja? I can use it in my column."

"Maybe you can help." Merril reached into her satchel and pulled out the picture postcard. "This is my great-uncle. He left home and came to Texas. Everyone thinks this looks like your courthouse."

"He left under a dark cloud," Vera piped in, "Merril doesn't even know his name."

"Is that true, dear?"

Merril was about to answer when Vera continued, "No one is allowed to speak . . . his . . . name."

"That may not be entirely true, Vera. No one speaks his name, but I'm not sure whether we're not allowed to or just whether no one does."

"I am quite certain that it is the former," Vera proclaimed.

"And I admit to being intrigued. May I see your photograph?" Effie Floyd reached toward Merril.

Merril passed her postcard across the table. Miz Floyd took off her glasses and stared at it a long time. It was quiet for the first time since our arrival. She put her glasses back on and stared at it even longer. Everyone else leaned forward and stared at Miz Floyd.

"Oh, my dear, that's a familiar face."

"It is?" several, including Doc, exclaimed. Merril looked to be tearing up.

"If I'm not mistaken, that's the damnyankee. Why can't I call his name? He was younger than I and had a right peculiar name. Doc, don't you know him?"

"No, Effie, he's a stranger to me." Doc did not add that Effie had a good twenty or twenty-five years on him because that would fall outside the bounds of buttering up.

"Well, if you think long enough, you may remember. This'll drive me crazy. For years after he left, people just called him the damnyankee. My brothers knew him better than I. They were about the same age."

"Do you remember them talking about him?" asked Merril.

"Not much in particular. I do recollect that all the young girls including my baby sister were just mad for him."

"I can see why." Vera had developed a crush on the boy in the photograph.

"My yes. He was a handsome fellow, and all the local boys were jealous," Effie chortled. "I believe it must have run him out of town."

"Why do you say that?" said Merril.

"To the best of my memory, he left town in a hurry. One day he was here, the next day he was gone."

"Well that sounds about right considering his previous history of doing just that. Miz Effie, do you know when that was?" asked Merril.

"I believe it was right before the war. For some reason, I remember hearing rumors about fighting with or agin' Pancho Villa. Likely, it wasn't any of that. He probably just headed for greener pastures. Funny how memory works. Come to think of it, there may be something about him in the papers. I surely wish I could remember his name. Was his last name Reynolds?"

"I suppose it's Reynolds. Of course, it could be Hall. I think that was my grandmother's maiden name."

Everyone seemed a little stunned. I wasn't sure if folks were stunned because Miz Floyd might have known Merril's great-uncle or because Merril wasn't absolutely sure of her grandmother's maiden name or which side of the family her uncle was on. No one needed to be reminded that she wasn't from around here.

"I'm so sorry, but neither of those names are ringing a bell . . . maybe something in the papers would help." Effie pursed her lips and looked toward the ceiling as though the name might be written up there.

Granddaddy took advantage of the opportunity Effie had left open. "Tell you what Effie, he said, "why don't we have the girls and Speedy split up. Some of them can take a look out in the archives to see if they can find the fellow and some can stay here with us, and you can tell them more about the history of the county," "Weren't y'all trying to write something about ghost stories and mysteries? Effie probably knows more about unsolved crimes than anybody around here."

Sister, Merril, Vera, and I excused ourselves to go out to the shed and go through the archives. Granddaddy, Lee, Winnie, and Susie B. stayed at the dining room table. Before we left, Winnie gave us strict instructions to be systematic and thorough as we went through the papers. She did not have to tell us that identifying Merril's uncle was important to the project, but not as important as finding information on Tom. Winnie had prepared questions for Miz Floyd that she hoped would get the information we needed to lead us to Tom. She didn't think it was a good idea to start with, "Aunt Jewel was having the table talk . . ." That's the way Sister would have started off. Winnie thought that we would be taken more seriously if she asked about local legends, crimes and mysteries and then steered the conversation toward Tom. Winnie was probably right. As we headed through the kitchen, Miz Floyd was beginning a recitation of local residents who were kin to Bonnie and Clyde and had helped them hide when the law from five states was looking for them. Miz Floyd raised her voice and said, "The key is on a nail to the far side of the icebox." It was on a key ring with enough keys to open half the stores in Mayhaw. Sister went back in the dining room to get Miz Floyd to help sort them out. "This is the one. Once you get the lock off, send Speedy back with the key. I don't want y'all to lose it. I'll be sure to give Winnie a copy before y'all go."

The shed wasn't so much a shed as a medium-sized barn. All it needed was "See Rock City" painted on the roof to complete the effect. It was almost bigger than the house. Sister fumbled with the lock for a while before it finally unlatched, then cut on the lights. I headed back with the key. When I got back, I faced several rows of bookcases just like at the library. The bookcases had wide shelves, about three feet deep, and were open to the front and closed on the back. They were about seven or eight feet tall and had eight shelves not counting the top. Miz Floyd did not use the top. The archives smelled a little like sawdust, moth balls, and dog food. The air conditioner kept the whole building nice and cool.

Miz Floyd's archives were well organized. She had copies of the *Stampede* dating back to when her daddy started it, stacked by year starting with the top shelf of the bookcase next to the far left of the door. The *Stampedes* went across each bookcase. When she ran out of room on one shelf, she started on the next row down until she had filled all the shelves on that particular case. Then she moved to the bookcase standing next. Once a row was done, she moved across the aisle and repeated the pattern. She added the *Trumpet* to the mix when it started being published in the 1920s until the merger, and stacks of *Trumpet Stampedes* completed the archives. Each stack of newspapers held six months' worth of weekly issues until the *Trumpet Stampede*. They were spread out more because it came out twice a week.

"Wow, they're in remarkably good condition," Vera noted.

"Winnie will have a field day when she gets in here. Let's just see if we can find anything about Tom and D. Y.," Sister said.

"D. Y.?"

"Damnyankee." Merril had figured it out.

"1914-1916 ought to be the right time frame. Have y'all noticed that some of these old papers are in better shape than the new ones?"

"That's because they have more cotton in the paper. It holds up better than the wood product used in later newsprint," Merril offered matter-of-factly.

"Are you getting ready for *Jeopardy*? How do you know that?" Vera was flabbergasted.

"I know some people who create handmade paper to sell in the shops back home."

"If the wood product of which you speak is pine, no wonder they are in such bad shape," offered Sister.

Merril concurred. "It most likely is pine."

"The ones in the years we need should be in good shape. Let's find them and spread them out on that long table in the back and see what we can find."

"Here's 1908, 1909, 1910, 1911, 1912, 1913, and 1914 right over to the top row. Hand me that step-stool."

Merril passed over one of those little red step-stools just about all of us had in our houses. The rhyme was near about wore off. You could make out the words only if you mostly already knew what it said; "This little stool of mine I use it all the time To reach the things I couldn't And lots of things I shouldn't." Sister gently pulled the stacks of paper forward to read the dates.

"1917 . . . Wait, did I skip something?"

"I don't think so. Look again."

Sister surveyed the papers again. "No, it just makes a big jump."

"Miz Floyd is going to have a stroke," I offered.

"Do we have to tell her?" Vera wondered.

"Check the case next to it in case they got swapped."

Sister moved the step-stool, stood on it, pulled the newspapers over, "Nope."

Merril, who had more at stake than the rest of us, said, "Before we give up, why don't we go through the years right around then and see if they got double stacked or just accidently mixed in."

"That's a good idea. Speedy, why don't you go up and down the aisles and see if you notice anything out of place. It may be that somebody just put them back in the wrong place."

"Okay, y'all, where should we start? 1910?

"I'll take the first half; Vera, you take the second half; and Merril, you take the first part of 1911. When we're done, we'll bring them back and start with a new set. I don't want Miz Effie thinking it was us who messed up her system. Speedy, if you move something, put it right back where you found it."

I headed up and down the aisles looking for anything that looked wrong—a stack that looked too tall or papers that were a different color. Whenever I'd see something suspicious, I'd carefully pull it out and check to see if it was one of the papers we were hunting. I never found one. Every so often, I'd hear them in the back of the shed laughing over something one of them had seen in the old papers. They weren't making as good progress as I was.

"I don't imagine I should be working on this project harder than y'all are," I hollered. I wasn't mad, and I knew Sister wasn't either when she yelled back, "Speedy, that ole bad man's gonna get you."

I finished my job and headed to the back. They were only on their second set of newspapers. They were making their way through them when Vera exclaimed, "Oh my word."

"Did you find something about you know who?" Sister asked.

"Or D.Y.?"

"No, but didn't the Titanic sink in 1912?"

"Yes, I'm pretty sure. In April."

"You'd think it would make the front page of one of these papers."

"It's a local paper, Vera. It only covers local news."

"But the Titanic—"

"Did not sink in Taterhead Creek."

I started helping them, and we looked through papers all the way through 1920 before deciding that we were going to have to tell Miz Floyd that some of the years were missing from her archives. Vera volunteered intoning, "It is a far, far better . . ."

"Vera, you are not going to the guillotine."

We filed back in, and Effie asked, "What all did you find?"

"Miz Effie, it's what we didn't find that's a mystery. The years 1915 and 1916 are missing from your archives."

She did not have a stroke, but it seemed a near call. She swelled up like a toad, her hair stood on end, and flames shot out of her eyes. "We'll just see about this. Come on everybody."

We marched to the shed—all of us—Doc included. Miz Floyd worked the lock. I was glad we'd been careful to close up the shed. She cut on the lights and headed straight for where the newspapers in question should have been. "Somebody boost Speedy up to see if they've gotten pushed back on that top shelf and the other papers have gotten in front of them," Miz Floyd ordered. We hadn't thought of that.

Sister and Granddaddy managed to get me high enough that I could see plum to the back of the top shelf. "Miz Floyd, there's nothing but a bottle rolled up against the back."

"Can you reach it?"

"Maybe if we get the front row of papers down."

They put me down, got the step-stool, pulled the papers off the shelf and boosted me back up.

"Y'all push me up a little higher. Miz Floyd, I got it."

"Hand it down."

I gave Miz Floyd the bottle. It was old and had some dried-up brown stuff in the bottom. Miz Floyd started talking even faster than usual. I couldn't keep up with what she was saying, but this was some of it.

"Damnation. That's what my brothers drank. They must have been in here messing with my newspapers. That just beats all. What in the world would they want with my newspapers? I'm going to kill them."

No one pointed out that Miz Floyd's brothers were already long dead.

A Visit to the Jail

We left with Miz Floyd still sputtering about her missing newspapers. Granddaddy promised her that Sister and I would come over and help her go through every paper as soon as Sister's summer project was completed. I'm sad to report that Miz Floyd did not refuse the offer even once, much less three times.

It was getting late, and Granddaddy said that we might as well stop for hamburgers at McRiley's. He knew that would be a popular idea for at least two reasons. First, the hamburgers were good–hand-patted from fresh ground meat from Mr. Baker's store. Second, it would keep us from having to recount the entire afternoon to Me-Mama and MiMi. A third reason was more personal. He didn't want to have to wait on his supper while the recounting was going on. As we were eating, Granddaddy laid out a plan. "When we're done, I'll take the Imperial home, and the ones riding with me can catch a ride with your Mama. Maybe you can sneak over and get the Do-doe and make a clean getaway. I'll try to distract Esther. Y'all need to be working on what you're going to do next, not what you've already done."

The plan worked because, as Sister said, "Doc is a professional distractor." The Altheans talked all the way home and late into the night about how they might make up for Effie's incomplete archives.

"Maybe the newspaper has copies," Susie B. offered.

"Effie Floyd is the newspaper. We can ask, but I doubt it."

"Nonetheless, we should check."

"I guess we also need to start looking at death records for people named Tom who died in 1916."

"So we're not giving up on this Tom business?" Lee was hopeful.

"Heavens no," Winnie explained, "the missing newspapers just add to the mystery."

Vera started humming the *Twilight Zone* music.

"I suppose you're right, but where should we look now?" Susie B. wondered.

"The courthouse might have death records for back then."

"There's always the library. They might even have newspapers."

"We might as well use a Ouija board."

"Come on. Your grandmother said that it was much better."

"Trust me. It's an exceptionally low bar. But we might as well give it a shot. Now that I think about it, we could tell Mr. Julian about Tom. He's a sport."

"Are you sure?"

"Mr. Julian taught us social studies and history in middle school. Me-Mama said that he retired after twenty-five years because he was tired of being held hostage by the state textbook selection committee. His wife still teaches art. He loves projects and mysteries." Winnie remembered him fondly.

"Vera, you'll love him. He's dramatic, too. I remember him acting out the Battle of San Jacinto complete with dressing up in a robe to show Santa Ana trying to escape."

"And how about the legend of William Barrett Travis using his sword to draw a line in the sand at the Alamo?"

"Victory or Death!" Sister shouted.

"I'm sure I have no idea what either of you is talking about," Vera huffed.

"We are not to be held accountable if your education is sorely lacking." The Texans in the bunch nodded in agreement. Merril looked amused.

"While we're out, we can ask around about ghost stories and mysteries. That, at least might get some results."

Merril said, "What if we asked your Aunt Jewel to have another séance?"

"You're not serious." Lee was not happy about this idea.

"I don't see why not. We could call it follow-up research."

"I would agree, but Aunt Jewel decides when she's going to have the table talk. She doesn't do requests."

"Unless maybe Granddaddy asked her," I offered.

"That's a possibility, but let's hold off on it until we've tried the more usual channels. I'm not sure how much of our paper can be based on sources from the great beyond."

"I agree." Lee was relieved by any glimmer of normalcy.

"We could hold our own séance!"

"Vera, I just don't think so."

"Well, I want to try. I'll lead."

"Of course you will."

"You mentioned a Ouija board. Is there one here?"

"Certainly, Vera. Aunt Catherine had a fully stocked supply for communing with the dead. They are in the pie safe. What color would you like?"

"There's no reason to be snotty. Do you have one at your house?"

"Every teenage girl had a Ouija board. So, yes, mine is probably somewhere at the house."

"Do you remember the time Mama used it and conjured up Martin Luther King at your slumber party?" I jumped in.

"What were you doing up?"

Before I could answer, Susie B. interrupted, "What did he say?"

"Not much," said Winnie. "He seemed none too pleased with all the screaming and running from the table."

"Do you think your mother would come run the Ouija board?"

"I really don't think Dr. King would be of much help with our present project."

"Besides, I want to lead the session." Vera was excited about the possibility.

"I'm for going back to those more traditional methods spoken of earlier," Lee was grasping at the most normal sounding procedure she'd identified.

"Let's try this. We'll go to the newspaper, the courthouse, and the library and chase down the leads we uncover. If we're still completely stuck in a week, Vera, then you can hold your session."

"All right, but I see no reason to procrastinate."

"It might take a week to find the Ouija board. I have no idea where it might be."

Vera responded, "That's fair enough unless—Speedy, do you know where it is?

I did not.

"Then that's a project for you."

Winnie chimed in, "Whatever we do, we need to make some serious progress. This project is going to be due before we know it."

Wednesday morning began with our usual routine. We would get up and figure out the goals for the day. I should say that Winnie would tell us the goals for the day. We'd eat breakfast and listen to the local radio station, KRJA, Keeping Rowja on the Air. Their favorite programs were the Community News, the county's social news; the local news, the county's real news; the Daily Devotional from the preacher of one of the hollering churches; and finally, Deaths of the Day. Winnie was particularly fascinated by the scriptural interpretations presented in the Daily Devotional.

Deaths of the Day was also oddly popular. It reported events scheduled at local funeral parlors. The program would start up with an organ playing *Just As I Am*. The song played for a while and then the volume was lowered while the announcer read the names, closest kin, and service information for the dearly departed. Then the music would well up again and slowly fade away before the commercial for Rest Haven, "Serving all your funerary needs," came on. The Altheans went into hysterics the day the announcer stated in hushed tones, "KRJA regrets to inform you that there were no deaths in the county."

Our first stop after leaving the big house was to the *Trumpet Stampede* to see if they had copies of the missing newspaper. It took a while to find out because the folks in the office had to catch up with Sister and Winnie. Finally, they told us that our best bet to find old newspapers was to check with Effie Floyd. They were shocked to learn that Miz Floyd was missing papers. The only other option they could think of was to head to Austin to see if the state archives had any copies.

"Do y'all think we should go to Austin?" Merril asked when we got back in the Do-Doe.

"It's a day driving down and a day driving back, and who knows how long it would take us to find anything, assuming there's anything to find."

"I'm of the opinion that we might do as well with Vera and the Ouija Board."

We headed to the courthouse and parked on the inside square. We visited a while in the courthouse and learned that we would probably have the best luck finding what we needed over at the county clerk's office.

The office used to be the county jail and was alleged to be haunted, so the Altheans were going to set up some ghost story interviews as long as they were there. We walked into the reception area and visited some more. It was important to visit before getting to business lest we be seen as rude. Vera and Merril didn't quite understand why, but they had learned to play along. Once Winnie had explained what we needed, the woman at the desk fetched Miz Minnie Collins, the perpetually elected County Clerk of Records. She came out, and we visited some more.

"So you are investigating mysteries and legends in Rayburn County?"

"Yes ma'am."

"And the first thing you're looking for is information on a murder that took place in 1916?"

"Yes ma'am."

"Do you have any more information that might help our search?"

"The fellow that was killed was named Tom."

"Do you have a last name?"

"No ma'am." No one mentioned that we might have had a last name if Uncle Parker hadn't thrown the domino out in the yard.

"Do you know if anyone was ever arrested?"

"No ma'am."

"No last name and nothing more specific than a year. Who told you about this?"

Everyone shuffled their feet and looked at the floor hoping for inspiration that did not involve tables.

"Oh, never mind. I can guess that Doc put y'all up to this. I suppose y'all know that he may have made the whole thing up."

No one felt compelled to correct her.

The record vaults were upstairs in the old cells. We trudged single-file behind Miz Collins up the dark, narrow stairs. The second floor had cells running along both sides of the hall. The hall was wide enough so a guard could walk a prisoner down the middle without one of the other prisoners grabbing him. Each cell was crammed with boxes that seemed to have been thrown in with no rhyme or reason. That is, no rhyme or reason to anyone other than Miz Collins.

"The police records and death records from that far back ought to be in here," she said as she tried various jailer's keys in the lock. "I keep telling myself that one of these days I'm going to mark these keys, but that day never seems to come. There we go."

The door swung open with a shriek.

"I'm afraid that the year in question is toward the back."

"Miz Collins, don't get your clothes dirty. Speedy, c'mon, let's move some boxes."

We made a line and passed boxes out of the cell. Miz Collins supervised the stacks to make sure they were kept in order. I was in the front of the line so as to deal with the majority of the dust and the spiders. It was better than throwing hay off the back of the truck. Even so, I was excited to uncover a promising box. "This here one is labeled: Arrests 1910-1919."

"Outstanding. Let's take a look. This is so much more interesting than filing deeds."

The last cell on the right held a desk and some chairs. Miz Collins fiddled with the keys again and got the door opened. This door was much more cooperative. I put the box on the desk, and she pulled out some ledgers.

"This one's from 1916, and here's 1917. We should be able to find something in here if they arrested anyone. Do y'all want to find some more boxes or do you want to see what we have here?"

The consensus was to look through the arrest records before moving on. Miz Collins began turning the pages. "What beautiful penmanship. At least we won't have trouble reading it. Some of these record books look like they were recorded by a chicken."

She paged through the ledger slowly. Periodic comments were made about some of the more bizarre crimes. "Oh look, Speedy, here's where Doc's sister Phoebe shot the cow."

"I didn't know she was arrested for that."

"It seems the charges were dropped."

"That's good. It was an honest mistake."

Vera snorted, "Your aunt shot a cow? And for what, pray tell, did she mistake a cow?"

"She thought it was Gillie Echols," I explained.

"Gillie Echols looked like a cow?"

"I don't know about that, but their daddy was off working fields on the other side of the county and their mama had taken to bed with a sick headache." Sister said, "Sister Phoebe was the eldest still at home, so she was in charge."

"Do tell."

"The story goes that Gillie Echols was sweet on Mimi."

"I thought it was Aunt Jewel," I said.

"No, I'm pretty sure it was MiMi."

Vera sighed. "It doesn't matter. Get back to the story,"

"Anyhow, Gillie Echols was no account. He'd hang around and generally pester everyone to distraction. Their daddy had forbidden him from the property."

"And this has what to do with the cow?"

Sister and I took to sharing the story.

"This one night, they heard something stomping out on the porch, and Sister Phoebe just knew it was Gillie Echols."

"And she hollered, 'Gillie Echols you'd best leave this house'," I added.

"And he just stomped around some more."

"And she hollered again, 'Gillie Echols, if you don't git, I'm going to fill you up with rock salt.'" I was enjoying my part.

"And he just stomped louder. At which point, Sister Phoebe grabbed up the shotgun loaded with the rock salt shells, threw open the door and fired."

"And hit Marvin Jenkins's Jersey cow right in the bohunkus."

"It scared it more than hurt it, and it went tearing back across the road to its own place," said Sister. "If she'd used the shotgun loaded with real shells it might have hurt it bad, but she was trying to scare Gillie, not kill him."

I shrugged. "Granddaddy always says Sister Phoebe claimed that she acted in self-defense."

"Marvin Jenkins was furious about it at the time because his cow didn't give milk for days. But he got over it once he found out it was a case of mistaken identity. He didn't have any use for Gillie Echols either."

"MiMi or Granddaddy could probably tell you more."

"That won't be necessary," Vera said. "Your recitation will suffice."

All the while the story was being told, Miz Collins kept scanning pages. "I've seen some arrests for murder and manslaughter, but none of the victims were named Tom. Are you sure you have the name and the date right?"

"Yes ma'am," Susie B. chose her words carefully so as not to lie. "That's what we were told."

"We have it on good authority," Sister added. She did not tell Miz Collins that our authority was Tom himself.

"I guess we check the death records next and see if we can find some sort of report there. Speedy, they ought to be right in the area where you found the arrests. See if you can slide the boxes around and see it."

"Yes ma'am." I pushed boxes aside until I saw one that looked promising. I picked it up and walked out with it. "I bet this one's it."

"Yes indeed. Deaths and Estates: 1910-1919. Let's see what we can find."

I carried the box to the office cell for Miz Collins.

"Good, it's the same nice handwriting," Miz Collins said as she turned the pages. She whistled softly to herself as she reviewed the names and the reason they had died. She moved her finger down the pages, pausing when she'd see a Tom or Thomas. She read until she'd ascertained that he had died from an accident or natural causes. There was one fellow who had died after being kicked in the head by a mule, but we all agreed that it wasn't a murder.

"It seems highly unlikely that a mule could carry out a premeditated murder," Vera concluded.

Miz Collins patiently turned pages until she said, "Something's been spilled—coffee, tea, Coca-Cola. I can't tell what. Several pages are stuck together and the ink's run all over the place. I'm afraid we won't be able to make anything out." She gently tugged at the corner of a couple of the pages. Her efforts caused some of the pages to tear a little. She tried easing a pencil between two pages to roll them apart, but that didn't work either. The little parts she could reveal were smudges of black ink on brown stained paper. "The best we'll be able to do is get past these pages and go from there to the end of the book. It looks like we've lost from about the middle of May until toward the end of August."

If Tom was in the book, he was in the ruined pages.

Miz Collins seemed as disappointed as we were. As she watched us put the boxes back in the cell, she said, "I'm so sorry we failed, but you said earlier that you wanted to talk with us about the building being haunted. I know I've had some unexplained happenings, and some of the others have as well. It's about time for lunch. But tell you what, we'll work hard here in the office and get things cleared off our desks. Why don't y'all come back about 3:30 or so and we'll tell you about our experiences?"

"That sounds great." Winnie was thrilled.

For once I was sad that I'd be at baseball practice, but I couldn't miss it. Our next game was with Reeb.

The Bluebonnet

The Altheans spent the evening writing up the stories they'd learned. It seemed as though everyone who worked for the county clerk had encountered some sort of ghostly presence—a cold spot, a glimpse of a fellow wearing overalls, a tap on the shoulder, and an electric pencil sharpener that seemed to have a mind of its own, to name a few. Susie B. even innocently asked if any of the ghosts had names, hoping someone would say "Well, Tom . . ." The folks who worked there had named some of the ghosts themselves, but none of the ghosts had actually called out a name. So, no news about Tom from the jail.

Thursday morning we piled in the Do-Doe and headed to the library. The library was in a brand new building. Hannibal had built a new library a couple of years ago, and they were acting downright snotty about it. So all the clubs in Rowja had challenged one another to raise the funds to build a library.

The old library building was terrible. It had been some man's house, and his family had donated it to the city after he died. If you're sensitive, you might want to skip this next little bit and catch up in a paragraph or two.

Mama said that the man had died in bed and that nobody knew about it until way later. She said his remains had eaten through the bed and then even started into the floor. Daddy said the family donated it because they didn't want to spend the money to make the house livable and because nobody wanted to buy it. Rowja wasn't inclined to put much money into it either. So, nothing in the house was level, the flowery wallpaper was peeling and stained, and the card catalog was in the kitchen in front of the sink. The roof leaked some, but it was over the bathtub, so that was okay. It seemed to me like nobody much even went to the library except to figure out where the fellow might have been going through the floor.

But like I said, once Hannibal got its new library, Rowja had to have one, and all the clubs you can think about tried to out-do one another raising money. The club that won the challenge had the honor of naming the new library. You never saw the likes of bake sales, barbeques, rent-a-teenager auctions, chicken dinners on the square, quilt raffles, dunking booths, cake walks, yard sales, womanless weddings and beauty pageants, fats versus skinnies basketball games, and drawings for products and services. Daddy took to bringing loose change home from McRiley's and dividing it up among all the cars because every time you got to a stop sign or the red light, somebody or another would come up and tap on your window wanting you to throw change in a bucket.

All in all, a passel of money was raised, and Rowja has a much better library building than Hannibal. In case you were wondering, the Garden Club raised the most money and named the library, the Lupinus Texensis Library. Most people called it the Bluebonnet. The only real drawbacks to the new library were that they didn't hold back much money for books and normal fundraisers were way off that year. The band hall still has a lot of leftover candy stacked up against the wall.

Sister related the story of the old library as we drove to town.

"That's positively gothic," Vera said.

"Of course, she could have been exaggerating. Not on purpose, but she's bad to combine what really happens with something she saw in a movie," Sister said. "Speedy, do you remember her version of the movie, *Rebecca*."

"Yep, she talked like it was the most exciting movie ever made. You and Daddy and I liked to have stayed up all night watching and almost nothing she said would happen ever happened."

"They were showing it late one night on the Superstation out of Atlanta, and the three of us just had to see it."

"Mama didn't stay up because she'd already seen it."

"After about midnight, they started playing ten minute long sets of commercials for every five minutes of movie."

"I still remember the phone number for the Incredible Bamboo Steamer."

"There was just enough of her story in the movie or enough of the movie in her story to keep us waiting for the rest to happen."

"*Rebecca*'s a good movie," Vera interjected.

"Not as good as Mama's version."

"Daddy eventually figured out that she'd taken *Rebecca* and a whole lot of other movies and created her own plot."

"What were some of the movies?"

"To be fair, the house did catch on fire."

"But there wasn't a crazy woman in the attic trying to kill people."

"That was either *Jane Eyre* or *Psycho* or both."

"And then there was something about a haunted picture."

"That was either *Laura* or *Dorian Gray*."

"What about the woman who was trying to drive the husband crazy and the man who was trying to kill his wife?"

"*Gaslight* and *Dial M for Murder*."

"And then sometime between two and three in the morning, the house burned down, and it was over without half of what was supposed to happen happening."

"The moral of this story is that Mama may have slightly exaggerated how the city got the house the old library was in."

"I, for one, believe that your mother may have missed her calling in life."

"She likely would agree with you."

About that time we pulled up to the Bluebonnet and piled out of the Do-Doe. As we filed in the front door, I noticed that this library did not have the strange smell of the old library, something like burnt broccoli. I had braced myself unnecessarily.

"Halt, who goes there?" Mr. Julian shouted in greeting.

"Seekers of knowledge," Winnie, Sister, and I responded and laughed.

"Enter," he declared. "My, it is wonderful to see you again. And, you've brought new friends. Do share introductions."

We spent the next few minutes introducing Altheans and catching up. Mr. Julian took delight in relating some of Sister and Winnie's escapades. We carried on for a while until Mr. Julian said, "Your grandmother tells me you are working on a project. How can I be of service? And, please tell me what you have learned about Tom?"

Lee looked like *she* might melt into the floor.

Winnie noticed and said, "Lee, if anybody would be interested in the mysterious Tom, it would be Mr. Julian."

"Oh yes, I am enthralled. This is the sort of thing that can make even the dullest topic fun to read."

Vera gave Lee a good, solid told-you-so-look.

"So how I can help?" Mr. Julian asked again.

"Do you have any copies of the *Stampede* from right before World War I?"

"Mercy sakes, no. If we ever did, they were stuffed in the walls of the old library to block out the breeze. Have you tried Effie Floyd? She keeps up with all that."

Mr. Julian was horrified when we told him about the missing newspapers. "Effie must be beside herself."

We were all a mite surprised that Mr. Julian hadn't heard about it before our arrival. He must not have turned on the radio because it had been on the local and community news that morning. Miz Floyd had asked for people to search their attics and storerooms to see if they had any copies from that time period that she could use to fill in the missing issues.

"Do you have anything else from that time period?"

"Let's look. I took over this operation after I retired. I thought it would be easy and interesting and an excuse to spend the day reading. To date, it has been interesting, but anything but easy. The first thing I've tried to do is get the material in some sort of order. The previous librarians do not seem to have been familiar with the Dewey Decimal System or any other system so far as I can ascertain. I'm not all that familiar with it, but I know it exists. I'm bound and determined to get as close as possible. I can at least use the categories."

"Should we make it a scavenger hunt, then?"

"It couldn't hurt. I pick up a box, open it, and sort books for a while. Then I type up cards and put them in the catalog. My wife Mildred writes the number on the binding in India ink or Liquid Paper. Then we put them on the appropriate shelf. I don't know what I'm going to do if we're not finished before school takes up again and she goes back to teaching more budding young Picassos and Pollocks."

"What happens when somebody wants to check out a book?"

"Fortunately, to date, we've had very few patrons. People are being considerate of our situation. If someone wants a book, we try to steer them to the areas we've already organized, but if they insist we let them open a box or two. They usually play out pretty quickly. If they happen to find something they like we let them keep it for a couple of weeks. We write down all their information in a composition notebook and issue a library card."

"Gosh, I don't remember ever having a library card."

"That's because we didn't have any. Mildred's gone grocery shopping, but she'll be happy to write you one when she gets back."

"Mr. Julian, I hate to say this, but it looks like you need our help more than we need yours," Susie B. observed.

"I cannot say I disagree, but you need to work on your project, not engage in the Battle of the Bluebonnet."

"Isn't there anything we could do that would help all of us? Speedy is real good at doing inventory at the store."

And Sister is real good at offering my services, I thought to myself.

Winnie looked around the main library room. Bookshelves were lined up with some random books scattered here and there. "Mr. Julian," she asked, "where are the rest of the books?"

"Stacked up in what will become the Children's Area, but is now deemed the Deathtrap. There were a few boxes in the storage and work rooms, but we cleared them out first so we could actually perform work in the workroom. Once we're done we will stage a grand opening."

About that time, Miz Julian walked in. "Millie," said Mr. Julian, "we have guests who are willing to help." We went through the customary round of greetings and introductions.

"They need information from the library to solve the mystery at the heart of their summer project," he explained.

"Oh dear. Have they seen the Children's Room?"

"Not as yet; however, our intrepid friends have offered their services to help us so that we may help them."

"That is such a generous offer. Are you children sure?" Anyone still in any sort of school was considered a child.

Sister declared, "We can start now and run home and grab some dinner and let Me-Mama know we won't be watching the stories for a couple of days. She'll quibble a little, but knows that our project comes first."

"So what can we do?" Winnie offered.

"The books are in boxes. The boxes are labeled, but the labels are general—science, fiction, children's, history, Bibles, Reader's Digest Condensed—we seem to have a lot of those–how-to, art, and so on. My greatest trepidation is reserved for boxes branded Other. You may also notice that the volunteers who moved the boxes did so in a less than predictable fashion. As such, any art books appearing together, for example, are more by happenstance than design."

Miz Julian broke in, "To be fair, the art books in the previous library were probably not together. Come and see."

Miz Julian opened the door to the Children's Room. Stacks of boxes lined the walls. Box towers teetered throughout the middle of the room. "Be careful not to trip over the tiny tables and chairs. They add an extra dimension of excitement to the maze."

"Wow," Winnie sighed. The rest of us just stared. It was an impressive display made even more so because the books were all packed in boxes from package stores.

"Does anyone else find it disturbing that Bibles are packed in a Boone's Farm box?" Lee asked.

"How much do people in this town drink?" Vera exclaimed.

Mr. Julian shook his head. "We make a concentrated effort to keep children out of the Children's Room. As you can see, this is a task worthy of Sisyphus. We would surely appreciate any help, but understand that your priority is with your project."

Winnie thought out loud, "What if we concentrated on the boxes marked 'history.' They might be our best bet at finding something we could use. We could pull some of them out, help get them sorted, and see where we stand."

"That would be wonderful."

"One good thing is that we can read the labels on all the boxes. At least we won't have to be unstacking them to see what category they fall into."

"Winnie, how do you think we should tackle this?"

"Mr. and Miz Julian, you should continue typing cards and labeling the books. Vera, you and Merril put the completed books on the shelves. Speedy, you, Sister, and Lee locate the boxes and bring them to the workroom. Susie B. and I will open the boxes and sort the books for the Julians." Winnie was in her element. "Does that sound good?"

"If it doesn't work, we can reorganize later, and if a group runs out of work, they can help another group."

"Mr. Julian, how would you like us to organize the books?"

"I've been putting the history books into the subsets of world, U.S., Southern, Texas, and local."

"We'll try to follow that pattern. If we have any questions, we'll ask."

"That will be fine, but your assessment is likely to be every bit as good as ours." Mr. Julian smiled. "Oh, and you may find that the books in a box are not necessarily what they purport to be."

We must have looked puzzled.

"The other day Millie opened a history box and found *Moby Dick* and the *Last of the Mohicans*. When, not if, that happens, place it in the corner, and we'll deal with it later."

We began working. Miz Julian showed Vera and Merril where the books should be shelved and told them that they had been organizing alphabetically by first author within each category. Vera and Merril began with the books the Julians had processed, but not shelved. Miz Julian checked their work and pronounced herself highly impressed. It probably wasn't up to national standards, but it was a durn sight better than the old library.

Winnie's system worked well. The hardest part we encountered was getting out the history boxes without tumping over the towers. The Julians were thrilled at the progress we were making. It was looking like we'd have all the history books located and sorted by the end of the day. Winnie helped with the Althea project by pulling aside books she thought looked promising.

"Y'all look here," Sister called from a back corner. "There's some boxes marked local. We might could find something useful in them."

The local boxes held all kinds of things—local history, church cookbooks, high school annuals, folk remedies, and a couple of telephone books. Toward the end of the day, Sister took me to ball practice, so I had to wait until the next day to see what they'd uncovered.

The Julians Find a Treasure Map

The next day, we listened to our radio programs and headed to the Bluebonnet. The Julians were already working and had a surprise for us. "We came back after supper and went through the books and located the ones we thought would be most helpful."

"Y'all didn't have to do that."

"We wanted to. You all have performed noble, admirable service to the Cause Bluebonnet and now should do your own work. We will continue to type cards and label books while you use the tables in the front. Simply alert us if the rare sighting of librarious patronicus occurs."

"All right, but at least let Speedy help you shelve the books while we go through the things you've found."

"Fair enough. Now come let me show you our treasures."

We went to the storeroom where the Julians' had stacked several books. "As you know, we obtain many books remaindered from yard sales." The Julians collection included a couple of diaries and high school yearbooks from 1914, 1915, and 1919. It also included an oversized volume entitled *A Pictorial History of Burton County*. Rayburn County had been named Burton County before Mr. Sam came along. It was renamed to honor him because as Granddaddy said, "There are enough things around here named for Beatrice Beall Burton, thank you very much." Granddaddy was a big supporter of Sam Rayburn.

The Julians had also found some genealogies of local families. Everyone was oohing and aahing over the collection when Mr. Julian declared, "And here's the piece de resistance." He held a folded sheet of paper. He carried it to a library table in the main room and began to unfold it. His treasure turned out to be a large, detailed map of Burton County. He had no idea how old it was, "It was folded up inside the Official Atlas of the Civil War. Given that nary a shot was fired around here, I am confident it is not an original page of the book. Nonetheless, it is very thorough and includes all the cemeteries in the county at that time. Also, given that the newspaper and county records have been of no assistance, Mildred and I thought that perhaps you could locate Tom's grave, or at least report on the search for Tom's grave. Some of the cemeteries are historic in their own right and the headstones could make for interesting reading."

"This is indeed a treasure," Winnie agreed.

Miz Julian added, "We're afraid we can't let you take this map, but I went to the Chamber of Commerce first thing this morning and got one of their good maps—not the tourist maps. They are no good unless you want the lake or the courthouse. This map is much better. You can use it to mark the cemeteries, and it has updated road numbers."

Mr. Julian jumped in. "It looks to us as if some of the cemeteries appear to be on private property, but if push comes to shove, Doc can talk you into most any place."

"This is so great. We hope you didn't put yourselves out."

"Not at all. Just make sure we are duly acknowledged when you complete your opus magnum."

"We certainly will."

"These photos are wonderful." Lee was paging through the *Pictorial History*.

"Yes, we remembered when the Historical Society put it together. They asked members of the community to submit family photographs and stories about their significance. The *Trumpet* and *Stampede* also submitted pictures."

"As you can tell, some people were better about submitting the photographs than they were at providing the stories."

"There is something good to be said about a heavy picture to text ratio," Lee laughed.

Susie B. joined Lee, and they continued to thumb through the pages while Sister, Winnie, and Merril started marking cemeteries on the new map. Vera had settled in with the old yearbooks. She would occasionally read a sentiment or verse out loud for the rest of us. The Julians continued organizing the history books and I shelved them upon completion. We kept this up until Vera gasped, "Oh my word." No one got excited because Vera had been known to gasp on a right regular basis and with little cause. "You're not going to believe this."

"What?"

"The Klan is advertising in the high school yearbook."

"You are making this up," Sister stood to go over and look.

"I'm not. It's a half page right over Davis's Dry Goods and across from Rest Haven Funeral Home."

"Sure enough. 'Best wishes Seniors from the Knights of the Ku Klux Klan'. That's just creepy."

"Does McRiley's have an ad?" I was curious.

"Yes, happily not sharing a page with the Klan. But Speedy, that's so beside the point. Doesn't anyone else find it strange that the Klan advertises?"

"Can you imagine being the person in charge of selling the ad?" Susie B. wondered.

The Julians joined us upon hearing the discovery. "It simply must have been a child of one of those Neanderthals," Mr. Julian, a former yearbook advisor, disapproved.

Sister was fired up, "Why in the world would anyone allow such a thing to be printed?"

"Different times," Miz Julian sighed. "I'm certain some of the yahoos are still around, but at least they hide off in the woods somewhere."

Vera had been going through the other yearbooks. "It's in all of them. 1919 even has a full page."

Mr. Julian posed a question. "What should we do about keeping it in the library?"

Many opinions were offered and rejected.

"You could put them back in the box and throw it in the lake."

"Why not tear out the pages with the ad?"

"Write IDIOTS across it."

Mr. and Miz Julian finally stopped these ideas by sharing a lecture on the value of the first amendment and the importance of historic preservation. "Knowing where we've been and seeing where we've come, helps us know which way we should be going. Censoring a message, no matter how loathsome or ridiculous, runs counter to being an American." The Julians decided the yearbooks offered an educational opportunity. They would create a special collection containing "one of a kind" artifacts of local interest. People working on genealogies or other special projects could use them in the library but not check them out. Material would be provided along with the yearbooks to explain the significance of the ads in context. After a little more discussion, we broke for Friday dinner at McRiley's. Several of the Altheans ordered the salad plate. I stuck with hot dogs.

After we ate, we drove back to the Bluebonnet to work on the cemetery map. Lee and Susie B. stayed with the *Pictorial History*, trying to match photos and family stories with the group's ancestors. Every so often, one or the other of them would call out a name to see if they were kin to anyone. Vera had moved on to the diaries to determine if they had any ghost stories or mentioned Tom.

The Julians and I kept working on the stacks. Mr. Julian was even talking about making me an associate librarian. I'd come back part-time after the Altheans project was done and help him and Miz Julian get the Bluebonnet in shape for its grand opening. In exchange, Mr. Julian would tutor me in World History when school took back in. That sounded good to me because the teacher, Mr. Morgan, had the reputation of being purely evil. I was already promised to Miz Floyd, and Granddaddy would not likely let me completely avoid chores, but maybe we could work out a schedule. Baseball would end for me as soon as county play ended because I wouldn't be making the All-Star team.

We were working happily along when all of a sudden Susie B. gasped, "Oh, my gosh."

This got more of a response because, Susie B., unlike Vera, rarely gasped.

"What?" rang out.

"Merril, I think this is your uncle." She pointed at a photograph.

Everybody got up and hovered around the book.

"It is. It is!" Lee was excited.

The photograph was of a good-looking young fellow sporting a bow tie. He was grinning like a possum and his boater was pushed back on his head. He was sitting between two girls, his arms resting across the bench behind them. The girls were holding up spoons and smiling for the camera. The three of them looked to be having a grand old time. Three boys stood behind them. They were holding bowls and staring down at the boy. Those three boys didn't seem to be having a bit of fun.

"I think you might be right."

"Merril, go get your picture, and let's put them side by side."

Merril hurried to her satchel. Everyone kept talking.

"Is there a story with this photo?" Miz Julian asked.

Susie B. scanned the page, flipped back a couple of pages and ahead a couple of pages. "It just tells about the importance of socials to the community."

"Oh no," Lee groaned, "I just read the caption."

Vera laughed as she read, "The Elliot twins and the Harris boys enjoy the ice cream social with an out-of-town guest."

"The Elliot twins look to be having a big time, but those Harris boys seem none too happy."

Merril was standing back holding her postcard.

"Bring it over here, and let's compare."

"It's nice that you can see more of his face. The cowboy hat casts a shadow."

"If you ask me, it's the same person." Winnie examined the photographs closely, "The nose is the same, and the chin is the same."

"And he has the same dimples," Vera fluttered. "He's so dreamy."

"Vera, you do realize that if he's alive, he's got to be at least eighty."

"Do you suppose he could still be living?" Merril had not considered this possibility.

"We'd need to determine his name before we go looking for him."

"We also need to find Tom and finish the project at hand before identifying further geese to pursue."

We all jumped when the front door opened. We'd forgotten that the library was available to the general public. It was Granddaddy.

"Julian, haven't you got a phone connected up?"

"It's supposed to be working early next week, Doc."

"I'm here to invite everyone to supper. Sister, your daddy just bought about a hundred chicken dinners from the scouts, and there's no way we can eat them all. Y'all come help us out. Julian, you and Millie are invited, too."

"Oh, I'm sorry Doc. We already have some chili made."

"It'll keep. Esther will skin me if you don't come along."

"We would hate to impose."

"You wouldn't be imposing. You'd be doing us a favor."

"It's such a sweet offer, but we really have a lot at home."

"I'm planning on cutting a watermelon."

"In that case, thank you for the kind invitation. We'll be delighted."

The Julians showed mastery of the rule of three refusals.

"So what are y'all working on?"

"There's a picture of Merril's uncle in this here book," I offered.

Granddaddy leaned over, "Well, so it is. Mmm-mmm-mmm. Those Harris boys look like their ice cream has left them with a touch of indigestion."

"You recognize them?"

"Sure do. That's John Bell, Jeff, and Sydney. I couldn't forget those faces."

"But you still don't recognize my uncle."

"No, darling, and I'm sure 'nuff sorry about that. And I'm also sorry to say this in front of you Lee, but I remember your uncles because I was strictly terrified of them."

"No offense taken."

"I swear they were mean as snakes." Granddaddy shook his head sadly. "John Bell did have one redeeming feature. He purely loved that Bertie. That's him there in that photo." He pointed at a picture on the facing page. "I imagine that baby he's holding is Bertie. She followed him around like a pet."

We were all trying to match the toddler in the picture with crazy Bertie.

"It like to have broke her heart when he died."

"Was that when she . . . ?" Lee's voice trailed off.

"I don't think so. It was before that. She was about five or six when she started carrying on. John Bell died a few years after that. Until then he tried to keep her under control. Jeff and Sydney—they were the worst—would be calling Bertie all sorts of ugly things and hollering at her to shut up. They tormented the younger ones any time they'd get a chance. John Bell was kind to the other children even if he was vicious to outsiders. I can clearly remember hearing him saying, 'Sweet little Bertie, don't be afraid. Nothing like that ever happened, and nothing's going to happen to you' every time she'd start out about spirits and phantoms, doom and destruction. She did get worse after John Bell came down with the Spanish flu. I'd wager that's when she got obsessed with germs, but she was on her way before then. Your Uncle Stuart took over Bertie's care after John Bell died, and he did a fine job of it. He just didn't have a way with her like John Bell did."

Everybody got real quiet thinking about Bertie. It was mighty solemn.

Finally, I couldn't stand it any longer and blurted out, "Granddaddy, the Klan advertised in the high school yearbook."

"Did they really? I'm not surprised. I recollect them marching and getting red mud all over their mama's sheets."

"Doc, do you really remember that or is this one of your Bear Tales?" Sister asked. We had grown up with Granddaddy telling us what he called Bear Tales. We weren't sure where the name came from. Sometimes he'd say that it was stories that went along with the *Three Bears*. Other times he'd say that one of his brothers would come back empty-handed from a hunting trip talking about how successful they'd have been if that big ole bear hadn't got away. All I knew is that they were made up stories and generally about dogs, not bears. He and Sister had made up this whole world of talking dogs, complete with voices and faces. They wound up telling them to me when I came along. Granddaddy would start off telling about an adventure the dogs were having until he'd get so far along, turn to one of us and ask, "Then what happened?" Me-Mama said it caused us to become creative writers with a general disregard for grammar and logic.

"I know I am bad to exaggerate, but this is the truth as I recall it. About once a month or so, they'd gather from all over the county and head into one town or another. They'd parade around like they had good sense. Folks mostly went inside until they left. Mr. McRiley would lock the doors and put up the CLOSED sign if he caught wind they were headed our way. Every so often there was some meanness, rock throwing and the like, but they were mostly just a general nuisance. They'd have regular gatherings out in the woods that were supposed to be a secret, but everyone knew where they were, when they were there, and who was there."

"Do, do you know if any of them were my uncles?"

"Lee, I guess I'm just full of unhappy news for you today."

"I'm not surprised."

"Yep, they, not your uncles, but some of them goobers asked me to join."

"What? When? You didn't?" Sister and I were surprised.

"There were some right prominent people involved. They told me I'd never get elected to anything if I didn't join them."

"Were you trying to get elected to something?" All of this was news to us.

"Naw. Some folks tried to put me up to run for mayor of Mayhaw back in the '30s, but I wasn't interested."

"What did you tell them? The Klan—I mean."

"You had to be right careful what you said to them. They were not renowned for reacting in a calm and thoughtful manner. Refusing the offer could have been seen as an insult."

"So what did you say?"

"I told them that Esther wouldn't let me." Granddaddy laughed along with the rest of us, but I bet he was serious.

"The invitation committee said that they'd have to go back and inform the Grand Gizzard of my refusal, but I guess he had heard tell of Esther—or he might have even gone to school with her—because nothing happened and they never asked again.

"The Grand Gizzard?"

"I swear it was something like that. He was some knucklehead from Reeb. I don't know," Granddaddy pondered. "He may have been a nice feller. I never met the son of a bitch."

A Visitor?

After discussing Effie Floyd's article, the Altheans decided to go through some of the books they had liberated from the Bluebonnet. The obituaries book was the most helpful. It collected obituaries from the Stampede and the *Trumpet* from 1900-1955. One reason it was useful was because it had a lot of information about everybody's ancestors–everybody's except Merril's. Another reason was because somebody from Rayburn County would die in a peculiar fashion and that provided a good deal of entertainment. Vera was performing a dramatic reading of one such notice, "And I quote, he was attempting to remove a fallen limb from the roof of his house when he removed himself instead," when out of nowhere Lady started up with a low growl.

"What is it girl?"

By now Buddy, who was not as bright, had joined in. No one was ever quite sure if Buddy noticed something or if he was just going along.

Lady's growl turned into a full-out snarling bark.

"Do you suppose something's out there?"

"Something's out there, but I don't know what." By now, Lady and Buddy were standing at the back door barking like fury. Sister said, "Turn off the lights in here, and let's see what we can see." She turned on the floodlights on the house and the outbuildings. We crouched down and looked at the back windows. Nothing was stirring. We stayed in a huddle as we moved from one room to the next. Lady stayed at the back door barking. Buddy followed us. We made it to the front hall and peeked through the blinds to see if anyone had come down the road.

"Here comes Peter." Buddy stopped barking and began wagging. Peter was heading to the house in a dead run. Sister opened the front door. Lady came flying down the hall, still barking, and shot outside.

Susie B. yelped, "Don't hurt Peter."

"Not a chance," I offered. Lady spun out as she kicked up dust, rounded the corner, and headed behind the house. Buddy decided to stay and protect the house.

"Y'all close that door," Peter shouted as he ran by. "I'll go check with Miss Lady girl."

Shortly thereafter, Pauline came riding up on a three-wheeler. We opened the door despite Peter's orders. "Y'all know anything?" she said. "Our dogs took to barking like unwashed sin and before we could settle them down, Peter saw y'all had turned on the floods, and he took off. I don't believe he changed out of his house slippers."

Everybody started talking at once about the barking dogs and trying to see something out the back window. All we could see was the beam of Peter's flashlight sweeping across the back patch. We went back to the front of the house to wait and discuss whether Buddy was a complete coward or a protective watchdog. Either way he loved hearing his name called. We speculated on what could have caused the dogs to act like they did and had worked ourselves up when something banged on the door. Everybody jumped; some screamed a little.

"It's me." Peter had gotten back. Lady was with him, and we let them both in. Lady headed straight for her bowl and began lapping frantically. Every so often, she'd pop her head up and survey her surroundings. Sister went to the icebox and got Peter a Big Red. He drank it down in two gulps.

"I didn't see nothing back there. Lady had done gone way down in the back patch and was right at the tree line. Whatever it was, she scared it for sure."

"Any ideas?"

"Naw, but our dogs was fired up, too. It was something or somebody. Do y'all want me to stay on the front porch tonight?"

"Thank you, Peter, no."

Pauline asked, "Did y'all hear anything that might have set them off? We surely didn't."

We looked at each other. No one had heard anything except for Vera's dramatic reading.

By this time, we'd moved outside to the front porch. "I'll come look around in the morning and see if I can see anything once it's daylight. If y'all don't mind keeping the lights on until we get back down the road, we'd appreciate it. We'll flash the porch light and then you should turn your outside lights off. If it comes back, cut them lights on again, and I'll come running." We realized that Peter intended on staying up all night to watch the house. No one argued with him.

Then Pauline pointed out something important, "I wouldn't say anything about this around your grandmother or Doc if y'all want to keep staying out here."

"That's mighty good advice."

Peter and Pauline crowded onto the three-wheeler and headed back to their place. Their front light blinked. We turned off the outside lights and made sure to lock all the doors. We spent the next few hours reliving the night's activities even though it was way later than we usually went to bed.

"Nobody heard anything, and nobody saw anything," said Winnie.

"Except for Lady," I said. She thumped her tail upon hearing her name.

"What do you suppose it was?" asked Lee.

"Most likely a possum or raccoon or something," said Sister.

"I don't believe that Lady would get quite so agitated over small, furry woodland creatures," Vera pointed out.

"Maybe it was coyotes or a pack of stray dogs," suggested Winnie.

"They would have probably stayed around and gone after Lady," replied Sister.

"I don't even want to think about that," I said.

"Do you suppose it was somebody instead of something?" asked Vera.

"I wouldn't think so, especially not coming up through the back. Once you get into those woods, it's thick. You really need to know the old cow paths and cut-throughs to get to a road. If it was somebody, he's probably lost back there," offered Siser.

"Such a happy thought," sighed Merril.

"Honestly, though, every so often, somebody'll try to break into the house because they've heard it's empty, but I think we would have seen or heard something—at least a car somewhere." said Sister.

Vera leaned back and yawned. "Maybe our mysterious visitor was Tom."

"Vera, that is not going to encourage any of us to sleep."

Reebers

I managed to get to sleep just fine, and there was nothing between me and the outside except window screen. I did encourage Lady to stay with me, and she curled up on the hooked rug right next to the daybed. She nosed me the next morning to let me know that Peter was in the side yard heading toward the back. "Mornin', Speedy," he called.

Peter looked happy and well-rested even though I knew he'd probably been up all night. I went behind the screen and pulled on some clothes real quick like, and Lady and I joined Peter in the yard.

"You the only one up?"

"I imagine so."

Peter and I began walking back and forth across the big house yard, looking for signs of our visitor. I had to step lively to keep up with his long stride. The ground was dry, so it wasn't going to be easy for Peter to find tracks. "There's some scuffed up places, but that might have been me," he said. "I wasn't being careful and was wearing my moccasins. The grass is kind of smushed up here by the back door, but that might just be from people going in and out."

He asked Lady to show us where she'd been, and she dutifully scooted under the chain link fence separating the house yard from the back patch and trotted through the back patch heading toward the barbed wire fence at the tree line. We used the back gate to follow her. The hay was pushed down where she stopped. "Still can't tell if it was somebody or just from Miss Lady girl working so hard." We located several clues that could have been something or nothing before heading back to the big house. Peter paused at the gate between the back patch and the house yard. "Speedy, did any of y'all leave that side gate open?" The gate was behind the old garage and apartment outbuilding. You couldn't really see it from anywhere but the very back of the house yard or the back patch, so we'd always been instructed to keep it closed to prevent livestock from wandering up to the house. The gate opened to a shortcut through a cow pasture to the chicken houses. At one point the pasture had been separated from the back patch by a barbed wire fence, but it had fallen into disuse after the family quit running cattle. If someone would have wanted to sneak into the house yard, it would be a good way to come.

"Peter, I just don't know. As far as I can remember, nobody's had any business back there."

"I generally check it when I come up here to mow, and I believe I would have noticed if it were open."

We strolled over to the gate but didn't find any signs of mischief except for the gate itself being open. Peter closed the gate, latched it, and made sure that it couldn't "up and open its own self."

The Altheans were up and fixing breakfast. "Peter, jeet jet?" Sister said. If you don't understand East Texan, she was asking, "Peter, did you eat yet?" and the question doubled as an invitation to breakfast.

"Yep, I did earlier." Peter most likely would not have been interested in bagels and cream cheese at any rate.

The radio programs were right dull that morning until the hollering preacher came on. It was the Right Reverend Miller Thornton from the Church of the Holy Apocalyptic Millennium. He was on some sort of a tear about how the *Trumpet Stampede* was promoting pornography and obscenity.

"I must have missed something," Vera called as she dashed to the front of the house and grabbed a newspaper. "I see nothing to inflame the citizenry," she said, flipping through the pages.

"Y'all, hush. I want to hear this." Winnie was amazed.

As we listened, it became clear that the Reverend was directing his hellfire straight to the pictures of the twirlers and cheerleaders who had been selected for the next school year. It looked to me like they had on the usual twirly-girly and cheerleader outfits. The twirlers were wearing toy-soldier band jackets with shorts instead of long pants, and the cheerleaders were wearing what cheerleaders always wear. For some reason, Reverend Thornton thought they were exhibiting way too much of themselves and the *Trumpet Stampede* had become a "purveyor of decadence." It had something to do with the end times and Babylon and Sodom. Gomorrah was left out.

He had frothed himself up into a lather by the time he started in on the Bible and how Timothy said women should be modest and be ashamed of themselves. Winnie had enough and scolded the radio. "And Deuteronomy 14 notes that we are not to touch the skin of a pig, but he isn't saying a word of condemnation about playing football." She muttered some more, but I couldn't make it out.

"Winnie, I thought you wanted everyone to be quiet," Sister teased.

Winnie was about to comment back when the Reverend Thornton changed his tune and said, "No, friends, we must look away from these wicked, worldly things and turn down the right road of truth and obedience. Let us look to Philippines to lead us to hope in these troubled times."

"Philippines!" Winnie sputtered, "We're finding hope on Pacific islands! It's Philippians, you . . ."

We couldn't hear what Winnie called Reverend Thornton because we were laughing too hard. We barely heard the phone ring. Sister composed herself and went to answer. She came back with the message that Me-Mama's stove wasn't working, and she'd asked us to pick up something from the Dairy Queen after we'd traveled to the cemeteries. Doc had a hankering for a steak finger basket. He liked the gravy.

We climbed into the Do-Doe and took off along the route Winnie had mapped out.

"You know, Speedy, the next thing you know the Reverend Thornton will be coming after you," Sister observed.

I blushed.

"And *why* is that, Speedy?"

Before I could answer, Winnie stepped in, "Speedy has always wanted to be the mascot for the Dirt Dobbers."

"Speedy, I think that's wonderful." Susie B. came to my rescue. "What does the mascot look like?"

"Honestly," Sister said, "the outfit is kind of sad. It's black and orange and has some kind of floppy wings and a droopy stinger."

I dove in, "Yeah, but Pauline said she'd make me a new Dirt Dobbers suit, and Granddaddy was going to rig a sparkler in the back so we could light up the stinger every time the Dirt Dobbers score a touchdown."

"Which is rarely," Sister interjected.

I ignored her and kept talking—faster, to discourage commentary, "and then I could buzz around the end zone with the sparkler making a grand display, but MiMi said it wouldn't be safe for me to run around on the field with my hiney on fire. So Granddaddy says maybe we could hook up a blinking taillight. He said it wouldn't be nearly as snazzy as a sparkler, but that a lot of the time the grass was real dry, and so even if I didn't catch on fire, the field might." I paused to catch my breath.

"Wow, Speedy. When do you try out for this distinguished position?"

"It'll be a while—only juniors or seniors have been mascots—but I want to be ready. I'm already working on the Dirt Daubers dance I'll do for tryouts."

"And on that delightful image, we reach our first stop."

As it turned out, we could cover a lot of ground in a cemetery in short order. Some of the cemeteries had nice neat rows of headstones, but some were downright snaggle-toothed. We'd each get in a row, or in some cases, what looked to be a row and just make our way across. When you finished a row, you just moved to the next available row. We moved way faster than the line for the roller coaster at Six Flags. We were mostly looking for three things—anybody named Tom or some form of Tom, anybody who looked like they might have been an ancestor, and anybody with a tombstone with an interesting message. Whenever we found a likely candidate, we'd shout out, and Winnie would come figure out if the grave was worth further attention.

That morning we struck out on Toms. None of the ones we found had died in 1916 or anytime near 1916. We did find a few ancestors' graves, and some of the inscriptions on the tombstones were interesting enough to be copied. My job was to write those messages into my Big Chief notebook. I'd put down the name, the dates, the cemetery, and the message. If a message was too hard for me to read because it had worn down over time, Susie B. or Merril would come over and help. They proved to have a talent for reading the tombstones with their fingers. They were able to make out most of what I couldn't figure out. If they couldn't and Winnie thought the message was a good one, she'd get some newsprint out of the Do-Doe and rub over it with some charcoal. We were grateful that Miz Floyd had arranged for us to get the tag end of a roll of newsprint from the *Trumpet Stampede* and Miz Julian had come up with several charcoal sticks from her art closet.

We were ahead of Winnie's schedule for the morning, and before we knew it, Sister called out, "Y'all, we need to head to the Dairy Queen and pick up the food. Doc will skin us if we're even a little bit late. Vera, can you drive? Winnie and I need to go over where we've been and figure out what's next."

"I'd love to. I've never driven a Do-Doe. It'll be an adventure."

"If it starts to shimmy, just ease off a little. It'll settle down. Speedy, ride up front and give Vera directions."

I pulled my seat belt double tight across my lap because I wasn't sure how much of an adventure Vera's driving would prove to be. I was surprised to discover that Vera's driving was way less dramatic than anything else I had ever seen her do. We made it to the Dairy Queen in good shape. I don't even think Me-Mama would have had to stomp on her phantom brake.

As we were pulling up to the Dairy Queen, Sister called from the back, "Go to the the drive-thru so we can all look at the menu." Vera dutifully pulled up to the menu board. Everyone studied it and called out their choices. I wrote them down because nobody could just order a Number 2 Combo or anything like that. I repeated the order back.

Granddaddy wanted a steak finger basket with extra pepper in the gravy. Me-Mama wanted a Belly Buster burger, cut the pickles and onion. Vera—a Belly Buster basket with ketchup on the burger instead of mustard. Susie B.—a taco salad cut the onions. Sister—Frito pie, cut the onions, but with extra cheese and hot sauce. Lee—a chicken finger basket with Tater Tots instead of fries. Merril—a cheeseburger plain, nothing on it but meat and cheese. Winnie—a Belly buster with barbeque sauce, cut the tomatoes. I want two corn dogs. We decided to get an extra order of fries, some onion rings, and some pepper poppers to share. We decided the dip cones would be a mess before we could eat them, but figured Me-Mama would have ice cream anyways.

I tore off the sheet with the orders and handed it to Vera.

"What is this cut business? Don't they always slice the onions, pickles, and tomatoes?" Vera was confused. Merril looked puzzled, too, but was more willing to go along.

"Cut means that we don't want whatever it is. Cut the onion doesn't mean slice the onion. It means leave the onions off entirely."

"You do understand that that makes no sense whatsoever."

"It makes sense to us and to whomever takes the order, and that's all that matters. Communication 101," Winnie observed.

By now, we'd been sitting at the menu board quite a while, so Sister directed, "Vera, go ahead on and pull up to the window." The window was only about ten feet past the menu.

"They haven't taken our order yet. I'm still waiting for them to come on."

"Vera, read the sign, or we're going to be sitting here a long time."

"What are you talking about? How long . . . oh." Vera finally paid enough attention to the sign to notice the piece of paper taped near the bottom of the board. It read:

THIS SIGN DON'T TALK

Vera shook her head and drove the Do-Doe to the window. She handed me back the sheet of paper with the order written down, saying, "I don't believe we share a common tongue." The window slid open, and I hollered out our order.

The Dairy Queen got everything right, and we had a fine feast. Granddaddy was especially proud that we'd gotten the pepper poppers. He allowed as to how "There's not much better than cheese fried up inside a jalapeno," when Merril and Vera turned down the offer of the last one even though they hadn't even ever tried one. Each one of their four refusals was spoken without hesitation.

As we were eating, Granddaddy said with a wink, "Vera, your cousin, Reverend Thornton, put on quite a show this morning."

"My what?"

Winnie sat wide-eyed and gape mouthed. The others of us got out tickle boxes tumped over again.

"Yep. Your Granddaddy's sister married a Preacher Thornton. Miller's their middle son. Come to think of it a whole lot of them Thorntons made preachers, most of a standard Baptist or Methodist sort. But there's a few outliers, and Miller's out somewhere past them."

"So I'm really related to him?"

"He's your Mama's first cousin. That would make you second cousins."

"Doc, they'd be first cousins once removed," Me-Mama corrected.

"Now, I don't understand all that removed rigmarole, but if that's what your Me-Mama says then it must be right."

The conversation then turned to how family trees were organized. Winnie thought it might be important for the paper, and Me-Mama was happy to teach her. Vera sat quietly for the rest of the meal.

I had to leave right after the stories to get ready for the game with Reeb. I was real nervous about it. Them boys from Reeb were big and mean and none too particular about playing rough. I ran over to the house, put on my uniform, and grabbed my glove. Sister drove me to the square. The team was going to meet up there and caravan over to Reeb. We tried to get there early, so we could practice on their field a little while. Coach also liked for us to go over the infield and get rid of rocks that might cause bad hops. Most of the other teams didn't worry about that sort of thing, but we did.

Sister didn't have to play center field anymore. A new doctor had moved to Rowja. This new doctor had got here somehow or another from Cuba and had been approved to practice medicine in a rural area. He joined the practice of Daddy's best friend, our doctor. Daddy said that Dr. Aldamo was a mighty fine doctor even if folks couldn't understand half of what he said.

Dr. Aldamo's son Chago joined our team because we were short a player after what happened to Tommy Austin. It turns out that he was a crackerjack shortstop, so Smitty said she'd be glad to move out to centerfield.

Granddaddy was excited Chago had joined our team. He was sure that Chago would serve to irritate the folks from Reeb. They did not approve of Rowja's United Nations approach to a team. Reebers promoted the principle of separate and unequal. The idea that we had girls on the team also caused great consternation. Reverend Miller Thornton's church was located directly across the dirt road from their ball field.

The Reeb team was strictly big ole white boys. Our team had black kids and white kids, a Cuban, a Mexican, and girls. A lot of families from Rowja traveled to Reeb partly to cheer and partly for protection. They didn't want us to be completely outnumbered. Games at Reeb could get pretty ugly. No, games at Reeb were guaranteed to get ugly.

The ugliness started early. Before the game even started, the Reebers were calling out all sorts of names. All of a sudden, Granddaddy started singing in his best church voice, "Jesus loves the little children, all the children of the world." The whole crowd from Rowja joined in and finished the song. Some of the Reebers were shamed into singing.

The truce didn't last long, and I was the subject of the first volley. I was batting second; as I headed to the plate, it began.

"Look at the shrimp."

"Y'all having to start midgets?"

"You're gonna have to change your diaper."

"Hey baby, your mama's calling."

Granddaddy had prepared me for their heckling and told me to tune them out and be more grown-up than they were. The folks from Rowja hollered encouragement.

"Go get 'em Speedy!"

"Don't listen to them. You can do it!"

"Smite them!" I had to smile when I heard Vera loud and clear over the rest.

I swung at and missed the first pitch. The heckling grew louder.

Sister yelled, "C'mon, Speedy. You know what to do."

All of a sudden, I *did* know what to do. I stepped in the batter's box, pushed my helmet down low, tapped my bat on the plate, took a practice swing, stared down the pitcher, and sank into a lower crouch. I walked on five pitches. Seeing me standing on first base, clapping, and cheering for Smitty to bring me in, sent the Reebers into a frenzy. I didn't care because I was the one on first base, and they were the ones behind when Smitty, who did not appreciate the names they were calling her—or me for that matter—smacked a ball clean out of the park, over the dirt road, and into the churchyard. She did a prancing run around the bases. I met her at home plate. She picked me up and gave me a kiss on the cheek. We waved to the stands as we ran to our bench. The crowd went wild. We were up 2 - 0 as the top of the first ended.

We were still ahead when the game ended early. Every so often, games would end early if it rained or in Burtonville where the field didn't have any lights. This game ended early due to mayhem. Our pitcher, Charlie Madison, had heard about being black all game long. Coach said to ignore it and keep throwing strikes. Charlie followed Coach's instructions.

After the first, we didn't do much of anything. We'd scored another run when, after he'd gotten the first two out, their pitcher walked me again and then proceeded to hit our next three batters. He hit Smitty just to get her back for the home run. He hit the next two because Smitty got under his skin when, on her way to first base, she yelled, "You think that hurt? You throw like a girl."

As the game went along, the umpire, Mildred Dickerson, a big-boned girl who taught PE at Mayhaw, was doing her best to keep control. We were up 3 to 1 in the bottom of the fifth. Reeb had the bases loaded because we had not done a good enough job removing rocks or had lost the ability to field. There were two outs and a three two count. Charlie reared back like Satchel Paige, and chunked the ball. When he let loose of the ball, all three runners took off for the next base.

Their batter stood still as a statue as the ball hit Betsy's catcher's mitt. He tossed his bat aside and commenced to trot down to first. The runner on third was almost home when Miz Dickerson punched out her right arm and roared, "Strike three."

The crowd was cheering and jeering. The boys from Reeb were slamming down their helmets and cussing up a storm. Charlie threw his glove in the air, and we galloped to our bench hoorahing about getting to bat again. We were sure to score some insurance runs.

Next thing you know, this scrawny little woman came charging out of the stands. She ran through the Reeb dugout, snatched up a ball bat and took off after Miz Dickerson, looking to club her in the head. We found out later that it was her boy who struck out.

Miz Dickerson was a head taller than the biddy from Reeb and was doing a good job of playing keep away. The woman was motivated though, and kept at it. No other fights broke out because everybody was so busy watching the chase. The ballplayers on both teams were pressed up against the fence so as not to get clobbered accidentally.

Coach took off after the mama. Coach tackled her, Chago ran up and grabbed the bat, and Sister and Vera dashed on the field and sat on her until Miz Dickerson could make it to her car and get away. Some of the calmer grown-ups from both towns got together and decided to call the game on account of not having an umpire and on account of nobody being able to agree on a replacement from either Rowja or Reeb.

The Reebers were none too happy, but it was one of their mamas who had caused the rhubarb. The two teams did not get together afterward to share ice cream and watermelon. We headed back to the Rowja square. Daddy kept the fountain open and treated the team to milkshakes. Mr. Smith, Smitty's daddy, took down the name of the Coming Attraction, and posted the score on the picture show marquee. Nobody from Reeb came to the picture show for a month, but Mr. Smith didn't care.

Daddy Tries to Help

Tuesday morning we continued to bask in the glow of the glorious victory as we split up to go to cemeteries all over the county. We decided to avoid the cemeteries around Reeb until we'd gotten the shoe polish washed off the car windows. We didn't think they'd necessarily appreciate sentiments like "Go Rowja" and "Wreck Reeb."

Despite our best efforts, we continued not to find Tom. We did have a bit of excitement when Lee found a Thomas who had died in 1916, but he had been born in 1842. All things being equal, he probably hadn't been murdered.

The day went even better than Winnie had planned. We covered our assigned cemeteries and even a few extras before heading to watch the stories. After that, the Altheans worked on the interviews Me-Mama had arranged, and I went to ball practice. I'm sad to report that practice wasn't very good. We were scheduled to play Burtonville the next Monday, and Burtonville was its usual sorry self. They hadn't won a game all year. Even if by some miracle, they beat us, we'd still tie for the county championship with Reeb. We'd represent the county in the annual contest with the champion of the county to the north because we'd beaten Reeb. Even so, if we beat Burtonville, we'd win the county outright and would be carrying a perfect record to play one of the Hannibal teams.

A team from Hannibal always wins its county's championship. Everybody says that they take the best players from the four teams in town to make up the county championship team instead of having a regular team play. Nobody is surprised that they cheat. Rayburn County is represented by its champion with no ringers. We didn't put together All-Stars until it was time to play in state tournaments. Even then, the players from Reeb wouldn't join if there were any black kids on the team.

Tuesday practice just wasn't what it should have been. There was a lot of clowning around. Coach kept saying that winning at Reeb was important, but that it didn't guarantee we'd win at Burtonville and that goofing off sure 'nuff wasn't going to help us against Hannibal. A few people shaped up after that, but mostly the excitement of beating Reeb and Burtonville's pitiful prospects outweighed Coach's words. Some people do not take baseball seriously enough.

It must have been showing in my face because when I got in the car to go back to the big house, Susie B. commented: "Speedy, you're not your usual chipper self. Is everything all right?" I explained what all had happened as we drove, and Vera observed: "Sometimes our worst rehearsals have been followed by our best performances."

I snapped back, "Well, then, we must be working up to a doozy." Their laughter made me feel better.

We were cleaning up from a cold supper when Vera inquired, "Has the Ouija board surfaced? The requisite days elapse, and Tom remains, alas, undiscovered."

"Oh, Vera, I'd hoped you'd forgotten," Lee sighed.

"Ah, treachery. Would you abandon this avenue of research?"

"Vera, it's a Ouija board."

Sister took a deep breath, and said "I'll go call Mama and see if she's remembered to look."

She was gone a right long time when she came back laughing.

"Well? What's the verdict?"

"I got Daddy on the phone."

"Uh-oh," I said knowing full-well that Daddy had good intentions but bad locating skills. He probably wouldn't see the Ouija board unless he sat on it, and then he might just think his chair had sprung a spring.

"He said Mama was out back working on her project."

Mama was known for coming up with projects Me-Mama called outlandish. One time she decided to crochet a rug using partial bolts of material she'd bought when the fabric store went out of business. By the time she finished the rug, Daddy said it weighed about two hundred pounds. It was too big for any room in our house, so she wound up donating it to the church. They use it in the fellowship hall.

Daddy calls her current backyard project the beer garden. Mama has decided that she wants a deck and a gazelle in the backyard. We were pretty sure she meant gazebo. So, for a while now, she's gone around to construction sites picking up scrap lumber and partial PVC pipes. She's used her electric chain saw to cut pieces to near about the right size. Daddy figured out that at this rate she'll have the whole yard covered over in five years. She never did like to mow.

Sister continued, "I asked him if Mama had found the Ouija, and to no one's surprise, he didn't have a clue. So I asked him to go ask her. He was gone for a right long time before he came back."

"Did he find it?"

"No. When he got out there she was running the chain saw and couldn't hear him holler."

"She's chain sawing in the dark?"

"Not exactly. She'd turned on the floods, so the backyard is lit up like the State Fair. Anyhow, he didn't want to walk up and surprise her while she was chain sawing."

"Mercy, no."

"So he went back in the house and cut the circuit breakers to the backyard."

"He did not."

"Oh yes, he did. He said she was standing in the backyard cussing in English and French."

"Good grief."

"She's so mad that he told me that he's just going to play like he doesn't know anything about it. She'll come in to check the breakers, and she'll just figure that maybe the breaker tripped when the freezer cut on. I'm to wait fifteen or twenty minutes and call back and get her on the phone. He figures she'll be calmed down by then.

"He's not going to tell her what he did?"

"No," Sister and I said in unison. Sister added, "And neither will we."

Winnie closed that conversation with, "Amen."

We piddled around a while more, and Sister went to make the call. She came back and said "Mama's found the Ouija board. She'll have it waiting for us on the kitchen counter. She also wants to caution us that if we have on all the floodlights while we run the chain saw, we should not run the clothes dryer because the power to the back part of the house and yard will cut off when the freezer cuts on."

"I'll keep that in mind should that unlikely configuration of events arise," Vera noted.

"Daddy didn't mention the dryer was running."

"I can say with some authority that he didn't notice it even though he had to lean over it to reach the circuit box. To be honest, I'm a mite surprised he found the breaker box and threw the right one. At any rate, the Ouija board is on the kitchen counter, and we are not to speak of the mystery of the lights again."

With that, Vera began rehearsing her fortuneteller act. We mostly ignored her.

Burn Ban Ends

We continued Winnie's plan the next day. She noted that we were making great progress in that we were ahead of schedule in covering all the cemeteries, but that we were behind because we hadn't found Tom, and we were running out of cemeteries.

Vera said, "Lee, you don't have to look so smug."

"I have to admit being pleased by our lack of progress in this particular area."

"Don't you forget, we have found the Ouija board and are not afraid to use it."

"I would never forget that, Vera."

We continued working our way through the cemeteries. The day was a mixed blessing because the wind that was keeping us cooler was also kicking up a lot of red dust. We were a mess when we got to Me-Mama and Doc's to eat.

"Y'all are going to have to rinse off before you come to this table," MiMi scolded.

"We do look a little like reverse raccoons," Susie B. said, looking around. The only clean places on our faces were the circles where our colored glasses had been.

"We need to get something next door anyway. Y'all come on over there. There's three showers so we can clean up and change in a hurry. I'll go ahead and run a load of clothes. They can wash and dry while we watch the stories."

"That should work as long as you don't start the chainsaw," Merril said agreeably.

Doc, Me-Mama, and MiMi had no idea why we were giggling so much as we filed out the door.

We got cleaned up as fast as we could. Sister said, "Vera, put the Ouija board in the car before we go in. I don't want to spend the whole meal talking about it."

"Aunt Jewel is okay, but a Ouija board is not?" Lee was confused.

"I haven't a clue, but I don't want to take a chance on a lecture that could be avoided."

We spent most of the meal talking about a different subject altogether.

"Al Bolton says we're going to get some weather," Mimi reported.

"It is windy."

"That thing that's been twirling out in the gulf has decided to make its way up here," MiMi noted.

We had not been keeping up with the thing in the gulf. "Is it a hurricane?" I thought the Yankees were going to jump up from the table and head north.

"Heavens no. It's just some sort of system that's going to bring rain. I think it has something to do with that La Ninner."

"We can use the rain."

"Sure can."

We pondered on the rain and whether it would affect our cemetery work. Winnie decided that none of us would melt, and we could continue as long as it wasn't a total gully washer or had lightning in it.

All of a sudden I had a thought. "We need to get Peter to cover up the trash pile."

"You're right. I'll go call him right now."

"Doc, you can wait until after we get up from the table."

"What trash pile?" Vera asked.

"It's that big pile of yard trash and dead limbs on the other side of the road that went out to the chicken houses when Aunt Catherine had chicken houses."

"Well, that is a remarkable mountain of trash, but why does Peter need to cover it?"

"So we can burn it," I piped in. "We can have a trash fire."

"A what?"

"A trash fire is when everybody gets together and burns a big pile of trash. You can start with just yard stuff and limbs and then you can start throwing things in it to see what color it burns. Hair spray cans are real good because they'll explode and come shooting out. It's real exciting."

"Speedy, hold on," Vera turned to Doc, MiMi, and Me-Mama. "Is everyone fine with this?'

They looked at each other, shrugged and nodded, surprised that anyone would be concerned.

I dove in again, "And sometimes plastic stuff will burn pretty colors. Sister, do you remember how your algebra notebook burned that bright purple color."

"I do indeed."

"This isn't a joke, is it?"

"Trash fires are a grand tradition in East Texas."

"Trash fires, not bonfires?"

"Oh, bonfires are way too sophisticated."

"And require permits."

"And fire trucks."

"I'm still not sure why Peter needs to cover up the pile of trash." Merril moved the conversation back.

It was my turn again. "Because we want it to rain enough that they lift the county burn ban. Right now we're in a burn ban because it's so dry that you might burn up somebody's house if a trash fire gets out of control. But you need to cover up the trash pile so it'll be dry enough to catch. Once it catches good you can throw some wet stuff on it, and it'll burn anyway because it's hot enough. It'll make a lot of smoke, but that's some of the fun."

"Wonderful."

"And you really need some good long branches or old mop handles or something to push stuff around in the fire to make it burn better."

"How close do you get to this fire?"

"You mostly get right up to it. That's the only way to make sure it's burning right."

Sister interrupted, "Speedy, what are the two worst words in the English language?"

"Burn ban."

"What are the two best words?

"Play ball."

Doc stood up, "Esther, are we done enough so I can go call Peter? It looks to be coming up a cloud."

"All right."

Doc went to call, "Hi-di-do, Peter."

"We're all fine. Listen, we was wondering if you'd go put some tarp over that trash pile. And make sure it's on there good."

"All right then. Let's talk about throwing a line in soon."

"Next Wednesday sounds fine if Esther will let me out of the house."

Me-Mama and MiMi cocked their heads, looked at each other, and snorted.

"That all sounds good. Our best to Pauline. By now.

Granddaddy hung up the phone. "Peter says 'hi-d'."

"Did he say he'd be able to cover up the trash pile?"

"To be precise, he said he'd already done did that."

Peter understood the value of a good trash fire.

The steady rain began during the stories. Daddy called from the store to say that practice had been cancelled. I was getting worried about the game with Burtonville, but they couldn't practice either.

Before he got off the phone, Mama picked up the other line with further instructions. Sister relayed them. "Speedy, Mama wants you to run back over to our house, and get punchos for everybody. They're in the ball game supply closet. She says to just grab the whole bag."

"Will do." I ran out the door and across the yards before it could start raining any harder. I grabbed the trash bag with the masking tape labeled "PUNCHOS" and headed back next door. While I was gone, Sister had already explained that punchos were really ponchos. She was currently telling everyone not to be surprised if Mama said that Dr. Byrd drove a Valvevo.

The Altheans worked on their interviews, and Granddaddy and I went to the back den to watch *Movie Macabre*, the booger show, on the black and white TV. MiMi came back one time, looked at the movie for a few minutes and asked.

"What on earth are you watching?"

"Gamera," I said, not turning away from the screen.

"What's it about, Doc?"

"I believe it's about a giant flying turtle that shoots fire out its butt."

"Oh, my stars," MiMi said.

After *Gamera* and the interviews were over, we took out to the big house. Vera was eager to get on with the festivities. On the way, Sister had an idea. "Now that things are winding down, we really should have some sort of thank you for everyone who has been so kind to help us. A trash fire and taco guts would be good. We could set it for Friday night. What do y'all think?"

I was all for it. "The rain's supposed to be gone by then."

"Taco guts?"

"The insides of tacos. You can use them in taco salad, regular tacos, or like chili. They are easy to make, feed a bunch of people, and folks love them."

"What do they consist of?"

"For every pound of hamburger meat, you put in a can of bean dip, then you fill the empty bean dip can with water and dump that in. When the water simmers off, they're done. Don't make a face. They're good."

"They really are," Winnie confirmed.

"Who all should we invite?" Speedy, write down the names unless you start getting carsick.

The Altheans started calling out names. Every so often I had to ask them to say a name over, but I mostly kept up and did not get carsick.

"Mama, Daddy, Me-Mama, and Doc."

"What about MiMi?"

"Absolutely."

"The Julians and Effie Floyd."

"The Millers and the Harrises."

Lee jumped in, "We'll need to include Bertie. It wouldn't be right to leave her out."

"Of course, she's invited."

"What about Aunt Jewel? She has played an important part in this adventure."

"Sure. I don't know that she'll come, but we should invite her."

"Peter and Pauline."

"Certainly. Can y'all think of anyone else?"

"What about Miz Collins?"

"Oh yes, absolutely. Thanks, Speedy. That would have been an oversight."

"What about Dr. Byrd?'

"Now, that's an idea. Do you think she'd be interested in attending?

"Interested, yes. Willing to hop in the Valvevo to drive over here for tacos and trash? That I don't know. It's kind of short notice."

"Tacos and Trash. That's a nice theme for the party."

"Back to Dr. Byrd."

"I say we invite her and let her decide."

"May as well. We can call with the invites in the morning. If you think of any others, add them to Speedy's list," Sister declared as we turned into the long driveway to the big house.

Ouija

Sister fired up some Spam for pineapple, Spam, and cheese sandwiches. Vera and Susie B. turned up their noses at the thought of it, but they liked it once they tried it. "I feel as though I'm gazing at Diamondhead from the sands of Waikiki," Vera sighed.

After supper, the time had come for Vera to attempt to contact Tom. We cleared off the dining room table.

"Should we try to make the table talk on its own or do you want to start straight off with the board?"

"Why don't we try the usual way first and then bring out the board if we don't get results," Winnie offered.

"Sounds good."

Lee sighed and closed her eyes.

"Lee, look at it this way. If we don't hear from Tom, we will be left to describe our futile search."

"That makes me feel slightly, but not much better."

The rectangular dining room table proved to be too big for us to have our hands touching, so we moved to the smaller, round table in the kitchen. The rain was getting harder. I thought that I'd probably have to make a Baptist pallet in the parlor because the rain might be blowing in on the screen porch.

Lightning was flashing across the pasture to the south. Thunder was beginning to rumble in the distance. The only thing that ever scared Lady was a thunderstorm, and she was beginning to get nervous. Buddy was just looking around like normal. Sister said, "We need to grab some flashlights. The power out here gets spotty during storms."

"What about candles?" Vera asked in a Dracula voice.

"We can try to find some, but about all I know of are some Christmas candles Aunt Catherine had, and I don't think the Clauses and Frosty are going to create the effect you want."

The lightning and thunder got closer as we came back with flashlights.

We arranged ourselves around the kitchen table. Lady crawled underneath and curled up across Sister's and my feet. Lee said, "Lady, I'm counting on you to let me know if anyone is thumping on the table." Lady tipped her tail gently on the floor.

"All right, let's begin," Vera boomed. "Are the spirits present?'

"Vera, they're dead, not deaf."

"All right, are the spirits present?"

Nothing except for more lightning and louder thunder.

Vera tried again. Still no response. The lights flickered.

"It's atmospheric if nothing else," said Merril.

Vera tried once more, "That's three. I suppose it's time to try the board."

Sister opened the box, "Do you know how to run this thing? We seem to have lost the instructions."

Merril jumped in. "Put the board on the table. You could put it across your knees like a table itself, but that's not very stable. Then we need two or three people to put their hands on the planchette."

"Say what?"

"Planchette. That heart-shaped pointer thingy."

"Oh. Okay. How much time did you spend out at Spook Central?"

Merril smiled and continued, "The one person asks questions and it should tell us the answers. Yes, no, hello, good-bye, numbers, spelling, and so forth. The other person protects against deception by a shady medium. Someone should take notes."

About that time, the lights flickered again.

"I'm finding this disconcerting."

"What, Susie B., the lights or Merril's detailed knowledge of the world of Ouija?

"Both, I suppose. Why don't I sit back and take notes?"

"Fine, I'm driving, or I guess, riding and asking questions. Who wants to be the other person making sure I'm not cheating?" Vera asked.

All heads turned to Winnie. "Fine," she said, "I'll take my status as honest board operator as a compliment."

After some delay in getting the board and hands arranged, Vera and Winnie were ready. "Don't put too much pressure on it," Merril warned.

"How do we start?"

"Try asking if the spirits are present," Sister offered.

"Are the spirits present?"

Nothing.

"Well," Lee declared, "There's our answer."

"Don't give up."

"Clearly, we have not made three attempts."

"Why is that important?

"Three makes it a scientific fact."

"Are you sure we don't need a more professional board? Maybe the spirits don't respect Wham-O."

"Just try again, Vera."

"Are the spirits present?'

Nothing, at first, until the planchette began trembling.

"Are y'all doing that?

"No," Vera and Winnie said in unison, their eyes wide.

"Try again."

Vera didn't sound so confident now. "Are the spirits present?"

All of a sudden their hands shot up to the corner. "YES."

"Don't let go," Merril counseled as their hands flew back to the starting point.

In a few seconds everyone let out a breath. Lee said, "Vera, this isn't funny."

"No, it's not." I'd hardly ever heard Vera sound so timid.

"I have to ask it," Winnie said, "Tom, is it you?"

"YES."

"Now what?"

Winnie was asking the questions now. Vera was quiet. "Tom, have we seen your grave?"

"NO."

"We've been to all the cemeteries—Black and White. Ummm, is your grave in a cemetery?"

"YES."

"In Rayburn County?"

"YES"

Lee Harris interjected, "I really wish you'd quit messing around."

At that, the planchette began moving in circles around the board. Winnie and Vera were barely hanging on. Winnie stared at Lee and spoke softly, "Tom, just calm down. We believe you." The circling stopped.

"Will you help us find your grave?"

"YES."

Before Winnie could ask another question, Tom started moving back and forth between "NO" and "U."

What do you suppose that means?" Sister wondered out loud. Everyone speculated on the meaning while Vera and Winnie were pulled back and forth.

"Maybe he wants to go through someone else," Merril offered.

"Tom, do you want to talk to me?" Winnie asked gently.

"NO."

"Well, that's that." Vera said, sounding more like her old self. "Somebody take Winnie's place."

"NO. U. NO. U. NO. NO. NO. NO."

"Vera, I believe he is even less interested in speaking with you."

Sister said, "Come on, Speedy. Let's give it a go."

I wasn't particularly pleased by this prospect, but wasn't going to be a chicken liver in front of the Altheans.

"Tom, what do you think about me?" Sister inquired.

It felt like the thingy was getting warmer, then it felt like it was vibrating, really more of a buzzing under our fingers. I looked at Sister. She looked at me. Before either of us could say anything, it near about jerked my arm off going up and back to "NO. NO. NO." It settled back to the starting point.

"What about me?" I was asking Sister, but Tom must have thought I was talking to him because he jerked it up and back, "NO. NO. NO." I have never been so happy not to be picked for something.

"Next?" Sister looked at the three remaining possibilities. "I swear we weren't causing this. Lee?"

"I don't think so."

Merril said, "I'm game. Come on Susie B. Let's see if Tom likes us any better."

"I'm taking notes."

"Oh, you should take a turn. I'll take notes," Winnie offered.

"All right, then."

We waited a little bit while Susie B. and Merril arranged themselves. "Who's going to talk to him?"

"Oh, for mercy's sake," Lee Harris exclaimed.

"I guess I will," Merril was game. "Tom, are you still with us."

Both Susie B. and Merril started looking at each other with the wide-eyed look Sister and I must have had. "YES."

"All right, then, do you want to talk to Susie B.?" Merril asked gently.

"NO. NO. NO."

"That's fine, Tom. How about me?"

"YES. U. YES. U."

"Ding, ding, ding. Weeee have a winner!"

"Vera, hush. Tom, am I the only one you want to talk to?

"NO"

Lee Harris narrowed her eyes and began glaring around the room. "I don't know when y'all did it, but I don't appreciate all y'all planning this to make fun of me."

"Lee, I am mortally wounded." Vera threw her hands to her heart.

Susie B. joined in, "Lee, I understand you are concerned about what people think about your family, but I wouldn't participate in such a thing. Something is going on here, and I don't know what it is."

Sister and I nodded agreement as Winnie spoke up. "I promise I was using the whole Tom thing as an organizing tool for the paper. I never seriously considered all this." She waved her hand toward the board where Merril sat patiently. Her fingers rested on the planchette. Susie B. had let go the instant she could. "Lee, maybe Tom doesn't even want to talk to you. We can see, and if not we can ask to spell out the name."

"You really believe this, don't you?"

"I suppose I do."

"It could be Aunt Jewel. He seemed to have a connection with her."

"We could just go over to her house. She won't even need a board," I proposed.

Lightning hit close; the thunder rattled the windows. Lady whimpered.

"It's too late, and we're not going over to Aunt Jewel's in this," Sister noted.

"I meant tomorrow."

"For heaven's sake, let's just get on with this. Your entire family could make a career out of tangents."

We laughed. It was true.

"Tom, do you want to talk to Lee?"

"YES"

"Lee, you're up."

"I don't think so."

"U. U. U. U. U."

"Please, Lee. At least you'll know for sure whether we're pulling your leg."

"We promise not to laugh."

The lights browned out and came back on.

"We better go ahead and turn on the flashlights just in case."

"All right, but I won't have you pushing this thing around. I'll know if you are."

"That's fine. You'll see." Merril was completely calm. The rest of us were eager to see what would happen. The rain began coming down in sheets. The outbuildings had vanished. The lights flickered constantly.

"We couldn't have picked a better night," Sister pointed out.

Merril and Lee arranged themselves. "All right, Tom, we're here."

"Is this thing always this warm?"

"Sometimes."

"What's making it buzz?"

"Tom."

"YES"

Lee shrieked and jumped away from the table, "My arms feel like they've been shocked."

We all agreed that was a good description of what we felt. Lee looked sick.

"Lee, come back over here, and let's see what Tom can tell us," Merril said with a strange look on her face.

"No. I don't think so."

"YES. U."

"Lee?"

"Lee moved back to the board.

"Try not to bolt this time," Sister directed.

"Tom, are you still with us?" Merril was as serene as Vera had been dramatic.

"YES."

"Good. Will you help us find your grave?"

"YES"

"All right. Have we driven past it?"

"NO"

"Ask Tom what part of the county it's in."

"Can you tell us what part of the county it's in?"

"MAYBE."

"Strange answer. Is it close by or out some?"

"Ask one part at a time."

"Oh, right. Is it close by?"

"YES. N. E. A. R."

Lee looked like she would throw up. A huge clap of thunder rattled the house. The lights went off and stayed off.

"I wonder how near."

"Are you within 10 miles?"

"YES."

"Five miles?"

"YES."

"Three miles?"

"YES."

"I feel like the Price is Right has a new séance game."

"Hush, Vera. One mile?"

"MAYBE."

This wasn't making any sense. Sister and I knew every cemetery around this area, and we'd covered them all. We said as such.

"Tom, your grave is marked, right?"

"YES"

"Are you sure we can read it?"

"YES"

"Which direction is it?"

No one quite knew how Merril was coming up with these questions, but they were good ones.

"S. O. U. T. H."

Sister and I looked at one another in complete confusion. She shook her head. Buddy stood up, stretched, and trotted up to the front of the house.

"Tom, is everything on your tombstone right?"

"NO"

We sat up. This could be important. We could have looked right at Tom's grave and never known it.

"What's not right?"

"N. A. M. E."

"If it doesn't say Tom, no wonder we couldn't find it," Lee mumbled, surprising us all.

"Does it say Tom or Thomas or something like that?"

"YES."

"Oh dear, there goes that theory."

"Is this why you wouldn't tell Aunt Jewel your last name?"

"YES."

"Will you tell me your real name?"

"YES."

Buddy had started barking in the front of the house for no particular reason. Lady was still with us, so we figured it was nothing important. Besides, no one was going to leave right now.

"Tom, I have to know," Lee joined in. She suddenly looked as calm as Merril. "Were you really murdered?"

"YES."

"Do you know who did it?"

"YES."

The questions were going off on tangents worthy of Sister and me, but no one wanted to interrupt Lee and Merril. They had fallen in a conversation with Tom.

"Tom, are you from around here?" Lee asked.

"NO."

"Do you want to go home?" Merril asked.

"YES."

"That's why we need to find you?"

"YES."

"Do you want us to find the ones who murdered you?"

"NO. D.E.A.D."

"It happened in 1916. Is everyone involved already dead?"

"M.O.S.T."

"Wow, I guess if we're going to find you we need to know the name on the grave.

"T. O. M."

A lot of things happened all at once. Buddy came tearing back from the front of the house. A huge bolt of lightning and clap of thunder hit together. The lightning lit up the house. Three of the Altheans and I screamed at the hulking dark figure outlined in the kitchen door's window. We flew in every direction possible. The Ouija board sailed across the room. Lady forgot all about being afraid and charged the door.

"Lady girl, hush up, it's fine," we heard through the din.

It was Peter wearing his slicker and large brimmed hat.

"Dang, Peter you look like an axe murderer."

"Didn't mean to," Peter barely entered the house. He pulled off his slicker and hat and hung them on the hooks over the tiled part of the kitchen. "I'll mop that up before I go."

"Oh, don't worry about it."

"I came to make sure that y'all was all okay. I saw the lights was out up here, and Pauline thought she saw some headlights leaving the driveway. We was afraid you was trying to leave out in this storm. We tried to call, but our phone's out."

"Oh no, we wouldn't try to get out in the Do-Doe in this mess."

"That's what I said, but she'd seen them headlights, and we both thought we'd heard some cars go back and forth down the road. It could have been the wind playing tricks."

We all agreed that we hadn't heard any cars or seen headlights or taillights.

"That's fine. I guess y'all didn't hear me tap on the front door. It made me nervous when nobody answered."

"No, but Buddy must have because he headed that way. Lady probably knew it was you."

"Yep. That old Buddy boy put his paws up in the window and pushed back the drapes. That's when I saw the flashlights and knew y'all must be in the back."

"Yes. We were just working on our project," Winnie reported as we picked up chairs that had been knocked over. Merril was on her hands and knees with a flashlight searching for the planchette. We found it on top of the icebox the next day, so our connection to Tom was lost for the evening.

"Did you do some good?" Peter asked.

"We made some progress, I think," Sister noted.

"Well, that's fine then. I'm headed back to the house. I told Pauline to get the law if I wasn't back in half an hour."

"Peter, can't you just signal her? We hate for you to go back out in this."

"I'll be fine. It's slacked off since I been here."

I looked out the window. Sure enough, the rain had let up enough that I could see the outbuildings. The lightning was north of the house now and the thunder had gone back to a rumble.

"It's a mighty peculiar kind of storm. I figure it'll rain on and off for another few hours, and then it'll be done before dawn."

Peter was confident in his forecast even though I was sure he hadn't watched Al Bolton.

"Look, y'all, I got an early call tomorrow with some fellers who want to get out on the lake. They figure the rain's going to get the fish all aggravated."

"What do you think?"

"I reckon they're right. We just got to find where they're at," Peter said as he put on his slicker.

"Lordy, I done made a mess."

"Go on, Peter. We'll mop it up. You need to get on home before Pauline sends the Sheriff."

"All right, but if y'all see or hear a car, flash that big flashlight."

We cleaned up best we could. Only having flashlights made it hard. The rain had eased off enough that we could open some windows to let in a breeze. Nobody said a whole lot. I guess we were too worn out to talk about what had happened.

Special Delivery

We spent Thursday tying up the last few cemeteries. We still didn't find Tom. The cemeteries were out beyond two miles south of the big house, but Winnie said we needed to cover them anyway, so we'd have a complete census for the project.

We'd agreed that we didn't want to get into our adventure with the Ouija board with Me-Mama and Mimi, but that didn't turn out to be a problem. They only wanted to talk about the storm. Me-Mama said that she'd been on the phone that morning with the electric co-op, and they'd promised the lights would be back on before we got back.

"If they don't get that accomplished, they might as well move out of state lest Esther take a plug out of them," Granddaddy chucked.

Me-Mama just shook her head. "Pauline is going to watch for them, and she'll go around and cut off lights and close the windows so we won't be paying to air-condition the county."

The stories were their usual Thursday selves. They went over what had happened on Monday, Tuesday, and Wednesday, and got ready for the Friday cliffhanger. Me-Mama had arranged for a couple of interviews.

Ball practice went a lot better except the field was mostly thick red mud. We were all covered before practice was over. Coach was hosing us off when the Altheans pulled up in the Do-Doe. They had been shopping to get the things we needed for the tacos and trash party. They were laughing as they walked up.

"Winnie, as a scholar of religion, do you know if a Golem is allowed to ride in a Do-Doe?"

"As a matter of fact, Vera, a Golem is allowed to ride anywhere he likes except on the Sabbath," Winnie teased right back, "and given that it's only Thursday, we don't even have to hurry home before the sun sets."

"What's a Golem?" I asked, dripping from being sprayed with the hose pipe.

"You can look it up in the encyclopedia when we get back to the big house."

That meant Sister didn't know either.

"Golly, Speedy, I hope you aren't too fond of any of those clothes. I don't think there's any hope for them," Merril declared.

Sister jumped in. "Oh, they go in the orange clothes collection, and Speedy can just keep wearing them to practice or to do chores."

It was true. We kept all our clothes until they didn't fit or until they had holes that made us look no-account. It was also why one of Rowja's school colors was about the same orange color as the stains left by the dirt. It helped with keeping the uniforms laundered.

I dried off best I could with a dog towel that was in the back of the Do-Doe. It was mostly clean. We needed to get on back to the big house to get ready for the party. Everybody we'd asked was coming except for Dr. Byrd, and even she said she wanted a complete report.

Me-Mama's nagging the co-op had worked because when we got back the air was running and the lights were working. Pauline had left a note saying that she'd made way too much chicken divan and had left some in the icebox. We were to warm it up at 350 degrees until it bubbled. When we opened the icebox, we noticed that she had cleaned out everything that might have gone bad while the power was out. She'd left a whole casserole because she was probably afraid we wouldn't have anything. She'd also left a green pea salad and a loaf of homemade bread. A pan of brownies was on top of the stove.

Sister went to call to thank her. There wasn't any point in arguing that she shouldn't have left us the whole thing. Pauline would have just said that it was all part of the security service and keeping us safe.

"I love Pauline," Vera sighed as we reflected on supper.

Sister agreed. "She may be one of the best people to walk the earth."

We spent the rest of the evening beginning party preparations. We got up Friday and continued getting ready. We didn't have any more cemeteries on our list, and Sister had told Me-Mama that we were going to be cleaning and cooking all day to get ready. Me-Mama always appreciated a party, so she knew not to expect us to come eat. We'd be having baloney and cheese sandwiches and chips for lunch.

Long about 9:30, Sister asked, "How long has it been since anybody checked the mail?"

We had to admit it had been a while. We didn't get a whole lot of mail out there what with Aunt Catherine being dead and all. Every so often she'd get something wanting her to take out credit or expressing worry that she'd stopped attending one thing or another. On rarer occasions, there'd be a letter from someone who hadn't heard the news. Mostly, though, the mail consisted of catalogues and grocery fliers. The only reason to check it at all was to keep the mailman from getting irritated that nothing else would fit. Me-Mama always pointed out that he was one of Doc's lazy cousins.

"Speedy, do you mind running down to the box and pulling out whatever's in there? We can probably just throw it on the trash pile."

I didn't mind even through it was a pretty fair hike. The mailbox was across the road from the end of the long driveway. The driveway was close to a quarter mile long. I was enjoying getting away from the school gossip as I walked to the mailbox. When I got closer I noticed the door to the box was hanging down, and then I saw it. I stopped, leaned forward, and started at it until I was right sure about what I was seeing. I took off running back down the driveway toward the big house.

The Altheans had been sweeping the front porch and dusting the furniture. They had stopped and were watching me charge up to the house.

"Speedy, what on earth?"

"Sister, I believe for all the world that there's a dead armadillo in Aunt Catherine's mailbox."

"A what?"

I had not mumbled, but repeated: "A dead armadillo in Aunt Catherine's mailbox."

"Surely not" said Sister.

"This I have to see."

All of us started off down the driveway. We got to the spot where I'd stopped and stopped.

"Well, sure 'nuff."

"How do you suppose it got there? Can they climb?"

"Vera, I am confident that the armadillo did not climb up the mailbox pole, back itself in, survey its kingdom, and die."

"If you put it that way."

"Has anyone ever seen a live armadillo?"

We talked for a few minutes on the subject of suicidal armadillos until Winnie said, "This is fascinating, but what are we going to do about the armadillo at hand."

"I don't suppose we could pass it off as party decor."

"It wouldn't be particularly festive."

"I guess we need to get it out."

To this point, none of us had made it to the end of the driveway much less crossed the road to get to the side with the mailbox.

"How? It's got to be nasty."

"I don't know. It looks kind of sweet with its head resting on its paws like that."

"Merril, trust me," Sister allowed, "it's an armadillo. It's dead. In a mailbox. In Texas. In the summer. It's nasty."

"Wait, don't they carry the plague?"

"No, leprosy."

"Also awful. I don't want to touch it."

"Do you suppose Peter could or would get it out?" I asked.

"Now there's a reasonable suggestion. We're nearly about to his house. Let's go ask. I bet he will."

We made a wide circle around the mailbox as we walked down the road to the little house. Pauline must have seen us or heard the dogs barking because she met us on the stoop. We'd spend the next several minutes visiting and bragging on the feast she'd left us. Then Sister said, "Pauline, I'm sure sorry that we didn't bring your pans and bowl, but we weren't expecting to head this way just yet."

"Oh, that's all right. I can get them tonight. We are so excited about the party. That's a mighty fine trash pile. I've been meaning to ask. Do we need to bring anything?"

"Just your own sweet selves."

"How wonderful. So what brings you this way?"

"Is Peter around?"

"No, those fellers he went out with yesterday did so good that they wanted to go out again today. I suspect he'll be home sometime this afternoon."

"Oh. We'll figure out something."

"What is it? Can I help?"

"Pauline, I don't think so. It seems that there's a dead armadillo in Aunt Catherine's mailbox."

"Come again?"

Pauline had heard what Sister had said because she was already headed for the mailbox to see for herself. It was just hard to register.

"Yes, that's a dead armadillo." We were lined up staring across the road at Aunt Catherine's mailbox.

"It would make a good job for Peter, but I think we should reduce the baking time as much as possible. We don't want it to explode."

Pauline's observation make me feel a little sick. This could be the worst chore ever. I looked around and could tell that the Altheans felt the same.

Pauline turned back, "Come on to the house, and let's call somebody official. That thing didn't just crawl up there and die on its own."

Heads turned to Vera who shrugged.

Pauline continued, "It was probably them fellers in the car we heard the night it stormed. I knew somebody was up to mischief."

When we got to the house, we began thumbing through the phone book looking for county services.

"Here's the number for Animal Control."

"Do you need to control an animal once it's dead?"

"Good point. Any suggestions?"

We sat around for a few minutes until Lee said, "Isn't interfering with the mail a crime? Why don't we call the sheriff?"

We decided to let Sister call since she was Aunt Catherine's relative and the closest to owning the big house. Pauline said, "Just use our phone."

Sister picked up the phone and dialed the Sheriff's office. We listened to her end of the conversation and tried to stay quiet.

"Hi. I, uh, need to report some, um, vandalism."

"Is this Faye? Well, hey, it's Melanie Catherine. It's good to hear your voice, too."

"Sure. Let's do that. I'm working on a project, but am free in a couple of weeks. Winnie's here, too."

"Absolutely." Sister put her hand over the receiver and said, "Winnie, Faye wants to go to Nacogdoches for Italian. Can you hang around for that?" Winnie nodded agreeably.

"Oh right. This is so weird, but somebody has put a dead armadillo in Aunt Catherine's mailbox."

Sister started laughing.

"I am not making this up. Anyway, it's in there, and none of us wants to touch it. Pauline thinks it might explode."

"Yes. I know. It is gross."

"Okay, I'll hang on."

Sister looked over. "She's getting one of the deputies."

"Well, hey, Dewey. I didn't know you were working there." Sister rolled her eyes. Winnie made a gagging noise that was most un-Winnie-like. Dewey was one of their most self-important elementary school and then high school classmates. When he was a junior, the senior class "will" left him "a sense of humor." Sister said that it remained in probate.

"Okay, shoot. I'll do my best to answer."

"Route 2, Box 14, Mayhaw."

"I don't know if it was alive or dead when they put it in the mailbox. I'm pretty sure it must have been dead."

"Hind end first. Its head is sticking out and resting on his paws."

"I don't know. It's armadillo colored."

At that, the giggling began in earnest. Sister stuck the phone between her shoulder and ear and looked at us with a what-do-I-say expression.

"I guess its most distinguishing characteristic is that it's dead."

"Dewey, I swear, it's an armadillo. Just send somebody over here before it explodes and the evidence is destroyed."

"All right then. Tell Faye 'bye' for me."

Sister hung up the phone and looked at us. "Apparently, the threat of losing the evidence lit a fire under him."

Pauline shook her head and said, "If they don't get on it, I'll have Peter take care of it."

Rayburn County doesn't get much crime in the middle of a Friday, so it wasn't long before two cars pulled up by the mailbox. We watched from the front porch. None of us was the least bit interested in helping. It took a while, but they finally got the armadillo out. Dewey and the deputy riding with him pulled down the driveway. The other car drove off.

Dewey got out of the car and swaggered up to the porch. "Would you come down and make sure that this is the armadillo in question?"

"No, Dewey, I will not. I am absolutely certain that the armadillo you pulled from Aunt Catherine's mailbox is the one that was in there earlier this morning."

Dewey and the other deputy interviewed each of us about "the incident." We agreed to the following: none of us had put the armadillo in Aunt Catherine's mailbox, none of us had seen anyone put the armadillo in the mailbox, none of us had touched the armadillo in the mailbox, and none of us knew of anyone who would want to put an armadillo in the mailbox. What's more, we could all account for each other's whereabouts during the time of "the incident."

Their next stop was to Pauline's house. She said later that they'd asked her the same questions. They also said they'd be back later to question Peter.

We were all just happy that the armadillo was gone so we could go back to getting ready for the party. We had radios on in several rooms of the house, so we could listen to music while we worked. Things were going well until they came on with "Bulletin, Bulletin, this is a KRJA news bulletin."

The bulletin was about the dead armadillo in Aunt Catherine's mailbox. They were even offering a Crimestoppers reward for information. That's when the phone started ringing with everybody, not just family, everybody wanting to know what happened.

We got so many phone calls that Sister assigned Vera to phone duty. She didn't mind repeating the story over and over. And, it got better every time she told it.

Trash Fire

Before I get to the specifics, I should report that the party was a lot of fun. The armadillo was a big source of conversation. Vera acted out the discovery and phone call. She did a mighty fine job of imitating Dewey walking up to the house. She did exaggerate some because if Dewey had actually called Sister "little missy," I imagine he'd still be picking teeth up out of the grass.

Me-Mama led the Julians, the Millers, Effie Floyd, Miz Collins, and the others on a tour through the house. She had a story for just about every room and could explain about some of the more prized possessions–the blue ribbons from the state fair, some of Great-Grandmama's tatting and quilting, her brothers' medals from the Great War, and other treasures. Miz Julian was most interested in the needlework, and Mr. Julian was fascinated by the medals. Effie Floyd asked Me-Mama if there were any old newspapers stored anywhere. Me-Mama didn't think there was anything other than the occasional article cut out for scrapbooks.

The Harrises stayed out on the porch because for some reason Bertie had taken to singing Christmas carols. Vera joined in on "Angels We Have Heard on High." They only knew the one verse and chorus, but Bertie was content to keep repeating it and Vera was content to perform. The strains of gloh-oh-oh-oh-re-ah, oh-oh-oh-re-ah, oh-oh-oh-re, gloh-re-ah rang through the air for the duration of the tour.

After the tour, everybody went to the taco buffet we'd set up on the screen porch. Folks ate inside the house and outside on the porch. The general consensus was that the taco guts were extra especially good. Mama said that she couldn't have made any better her own self. She also pointed out that she was proud of us for having the good sense to host the party to retaliate for everything folks had done for us.

The Altheans had apparently been plotting something because after supper, when everyone was sitting around talking, sister said, "Aunt Jewel, how would you feel about having a table talking? I'm sure some of these folks have never been to one." The Julians nodded enthusiastically. Effie Floyd, said "Somebody go get my camera out of the front room next to my pocketbook."

Aunt Jewel just shook her head.

Doc jumped in. "Oh come on, Jewel, I don't believe you've ever had one out here at Esther's home place. I bet her people have a lot to say. They always do."

Me-Mama did not look pleased at that comment.

"Oh, there's spirits around, but tonight is not the time, and I don't want my picture made."

"Effie," Doc said, "this table talking is strictly off-the-record."

"All right, but the party and the armadillo report will appear in the next column."

"There you go Jewel. You are free to contact Esther's people without publicity."

Aunt Jewel got a peculiar, far-away look on her face. She turned toward the kitchen and said, "Esther's people are not interested in talking to anyone tonight. There's other business here."

"Jewel, what are you talking about? Esther's papa built this house his own self, and nobody's lived or died out here 'cept family or in-laws."

"Only one spirit is interested in talking."

Mimi interrupted, "It's probably Catherine. Didn't she die in the same room she was born in?"

Me-Mama said, "Yes." The Altheans looked toward Sister silently wondering which room. Sister looked at Vera, smiled a little and mouthed, "Yours." Vera went a little pale at that.

Aunt Jewel turned away from Mimi and looked back toward the kitchen. "It is not Catherine. He is not one of Esther's people."

"So it's just somebody who just showed up. Is he just passing through? Seems to me like we need to know his business hanging around our place," Doc teased, "You need to ask him to account for himself."

"No point in it. He doesn't want to be here. There is anger here."

"Do you suppose he put the armadillo in the mailbox?"

"Don't be ridiculous, Naomi," Aunt Jewel snapped. "He's angry, but not at us."

"How do you know this?" Miz Julian wondered.

The Altheans and I were interested in this answer. We understood she was talking about Tom.

"I just know, and I also know that he does not want to talk to me." With that, Aunt Jewel turned from looking at the kitchen and stared directly at Lee Harris and then Merril. Lee Harris went completely blank. Merril smiled and looked over Aunt Jewel's shoulder into the kitchen.

About that time, the Harrises came in the house and walked down the hall. All of a sudden, Bertie stopped in her tracks and took to chanting. "Beware, beware, the sins of the fathers are visited on the sons. Beware, beware, angels fall from the sky . . ." It was the same thing she'd been doing at funerals all summer long.

The Harrises looked mighty chagrined until Susie B. said, "Bertie, why don't we go outside and look for angels still in the sky?" Vera added, "We can sing some more, Bertie. Doesn't that sound fun?" Bertie stopped chanting, looked down the hall into the kitchen, smiled and nodded. She headed out of the house talking all the while about taking care of the beautiful angel. Susie B. and Vera turned to each other shrugged and followed her down the hall. Sure enough, in a minute or two, "Hark the Herald Angels Sing" filled the air.

The Harrises took to apologizing for Bertie, but no one was all that worried. Granddaddy said, "It probably has something to do with whatever spirit Jewel attracted, so I blame her for any sort of carrying on."

"Doc," said Jewel, "I would not argue that the spirit reached out to Bertie, but that spirit was here long before I got here, so I did not conjure it."

Everyone was quiet for a few seconds. Granddaddy started to open his mouth, when Aunt Jewel continued, "And I'll tell you this, Sylvester Ferrin, the angry went right on out of that spirit when Bertie came down the hall. He felt kindly toward her."

Before anyone else could say anything, the front door opened, and Pauline walked in. "It's about dark-thirty. Peter's got the drip torch and is lighting the trash fire."

It was an excellent trash fire. Peter had done a good job keeping the main part dry, and it burned like fury. Doc, Mimi, Me-Mama, Daddy, Effie Floyd, Miz Collins, and the Julians all pulled up lawn chairs to observe the proceedings. They were joined by Lee Harris, Susie B., and Vera. The rest of us had fun throwing things on the trash pile to see if they'd explode or burn bright colors. We poked the big limbs and fence posts around to make sure they'd burn right. We'd shift whenever the light breeze would send the smoke and sparks in a new direction.

Every so often, Vera would say something about our "burned and charred bodies," but we mostly ignored her. Merril would laugh and say that she'd never done anything like this before. She was a natural at a trash fire.

I stared at the fire as it danced at my feet. I loved the way it smelled, mostly burning pine with a chemical undertone. Tonight, the smell would remain in my clothes and hair. My face felt hot and dry like I'd spent a day at the beach, and my eyes burned and stung a little. I could stare at a trash fire forever.

As the fire died down, people began to say their good-byes. Mama and Daddy had to be at work the next morning, and they had driven Aunt Jewel and Effie Floyd. As Daddy said, "Aunt Jewel doesn't drive at night, and it would have taken Effie Floyd until sunup to get out here." He did not say that within range of Miz Floyd. The Millers and Miz Collins had ridden together on account of Miz Collins not knowing how to get out here. The Julians talked with Me-Mama a little before they left. They were interested in writing up a brief history of the home place, and Miz Julian had taken a notion about drawing a picture of the house. Me-Mama said she was amenable to both and that they'd talk about it as soon as the girls had finished their project.

Before long, all that was left was me and the Altheans, Doc, Me-Mama, Mimi, Peter, and Pauline. Me-Mama and Granddaddy were going to spend the weekend at Mimi's house on the lake. They had no reason to hurry off. Besides, they enjoyed a trash fire with the best of them. We sat around in the lawn chairs watching the fire slowly die away.

"How much more do you have on your project?" Me-Mama asked.

"We've visited all the cemeteries and investigated all the newspapers and records we can think of," Winnie answered. "We're going to be able to write up a good history of our families in the county."

"Will your teacher be pleased?"

"I imagine so," Sister jumped in. "She gave us a lot of leeway. She mainly likes good work and good writing. I'm just disappointed that we never solved the two mysteries."

"That Tom fellow?" Granddaddy asked. "Do you suppose that's who Jewel was going on about?"

"It most certainly was. He was just here the other night."

"Vera," Lee Harris was put out. "I thought we agreed that we weren't going to talk about it."

"Doc brought it up first."

With that, we had to confess to the session with the Ouija Board and tell the whole story. Before it was over, everybody was laughing at how Peter had scared us. "Peter, I imagine they thought you were ole Tom rose up and looking in the window."

"Oh Doc, you would have screamed like a little girl and hid under the table if you'd been there."

"Don't believe Mimi, girls. I'd of stood right up and said, 'You old ghost. Go on and git'."

"Doc, am I going to have to tell them about the time," Mimi did not finish her question before Doc laughed and said, "You are not. So Tom's the first mystery. I forget the second."

"Merril's uncle."

"Oh, that's right. You're trying to find out his name and where he might have gone."

"Yes sir."

"Naomi, have you ever seen that picture Merril has? I don't recollect having ever seen the feller, but you are so much *older* than I am maybe you'll know him."

Mimi looked over her glasses. "Doc, that ole bad man's gonna git you." She turned to Merril, lightened the tone of her voice and said, "Merril, dear, I don't believe I have. I'd be happy to take a gander at it with my *ancient* eyeballs."

"Speedy, run in the house and get the picture and a flashlight. Be careful and don't bend it—the picture I mean," Me-Mama ordered.

I got them back safely.

Mimi squinted at the picture. "Speedy, come here and shine the light where I can get a good look at it. I can't hold both and get a good angle."

We negotiated how I should direct the beam a while before she was satisfied. She looked at the photo, moved it back and forth, and declared, "That's Roy."

"Roy?" The entire group repeated the name.

"Yes, Roy. I'm sure of it. All the girls were crazy for him, and all the hometown fellers were mighty jealous."

"I told you he was dreamy," Vera sighed.

"You knew him?" Merril was stunned. "You really knew him? And his name was Roy? Roy Reynolds?"

"I certainly did know him, but I don't recollect that his last name was Reynolds. Matter of fact, I can't recollect it exactly. But it seems like it was a funny name."

"Merril, he likely changed it when he ran off from New York."

"That just settles it. Roy was a Yankee. All the boys called him 'Damnyankee.' It might as well been his name."

"How did you know him?" Me-Mama asked.

"He was courting one of my sisters, Jewel or maybe Phoebe. Anyhow, he'd ride up to the house on a fine horse, not like that Gillie Echols and his old hard tail mule."

"Was Gillie Echols courting you?

"Not me. It was Jewel."

"Told you so."

"What else do you remember?"

"Not a whole bunch. He was around the county for a while, and then he was gone. I heard tell he joined the army and took a train. Esther, I believe your papa bought his horse. It was a big roan colored horse with white stockings."

"I remember that horse."

"Esther, how is it you can remember that horse, but you can't remember that boy's last name?"

"First off, that horse was around here a whole lot longer than he was. Second off, it was a sure 'nuff pretty horse. Third off, I wasn't very old at the time he would have been here."

"Do you remember anything else about Roy?"

"Not really, Merril. I believe I heard tell that he went to Fort Riley, Kansas, or maybe San Antonio, but don't know anything else. If I recollect his name, I'll tell you first thing."

"That would be wonderful."

We sat and stared at the embers and listened to the wood pop.

"I guess that leaves Tom." Sister let out a breath.

"Have you checked everything you can think of?" Me-Mama asked.

"Yes ma'am. We've hit a lot of dead ends, pardon the expression. The county records are incomplete, Miz Floyd's newspapers are missing for that time, and he doesn't seem to be in any of the cemeteries."

"Alas, Aunt Jewel was our best hope of finding him. She was neither amused by nor interested in the prospects."

"So that's what all that fuss was about."

"Yes sir."

"Well, I'd of tried a little harder, but generally once she's set, she's set."

Me-Mama asked again, "You are absolutely sure you've been to all the cemeteries?"

"Yes ma'am, all of them that there's a record of or that anybody told us about," Winnie declared sadly.

We sat and considered the fire a little longer. Finally, Peter stood up, stretched, and started over to push the remains of the fire in on themselves. As he walked, he scratched behind his ear and wondered, "Even that old cemetery on Taterhead Creek out there on the back of the property? Back there near to where that old bridge washed out?"

We stared at his back as he worked the fire.

Peter's Plan

Me-Mama looked puzzled. "It had slipped my mind, but I don't think it would help solve the mystery. Nobody's been buried there in more than a hundred years. I seem to remember some markers, but nobody's kept it up, so I doubt you'd be able to read them. Some sort of sickness came through Papa's family and those that came over here with them from Alabama. Doc, some of your people came through about then."

"Yep, my people would have constituted the hired help. And you're right. I believe the story goes that they buried them that died in a hurry and away from the houses. I had forgot about that cemetery, too, and that bridge was a shortcut to an old Spanish trail that ran about where the Mayhaw road runs today. That bridge kept washing out due to beaver dams as I recall. That land back there's rocky and swampy all at once. It's not good for growing much except skeeters, blackberries, and snakes."

"Fabulous," Sister shuddered. She did not care for any sort of snake. Neither did I.

"And part of it's under water if the creek's running high," Peter pointed out.

Susie B. tried to be helpful, "Well that rules it out because Tom said he's not under water."

Peter broke in. "It's not all under water. Just where it's done washed out. Part of it's still high and dry."

I believed I had a crucial point to make. "Besides, Tom said he wasn't under Lake Burton. He didn't say a word about Taterhead Creek."

"So true."

Lee Harris looked like she was going to say something, but just closed her mouth and sighed.

"The cemetery is washed out?" Vera wanted to clarify something Peter had said. "Oh dear me, Peter, are there any bones?" She looked a little queasy.

MiMi huffed, "Well, if there are, we can't have that. We'll need to get up there and bury them properly. We can't have people thinking we're shiftless and not respectful."

"I swear, Naomi, ten minutes ago, we'd all forgotten there was even a cemetery."

"So are there any bones?" I was interested. This would make a great story for the team.

"Nah. I ain't never seen none. I reckon they done washed down the creek a ways yonder."

"I ain't never seen any," Pauline corrected.

"Scuse me, seen any."

"Doc, you know the property better than anybody. How would you get back there?" Sister asked.

Doc leaned back, laid his hands on the table, and said in his most serious voice, "Girls, I don't rightly know. It's completely grown up. We don't even run the fence line back there anymore because it's all covered up and good for nothing to boot."

It was hard for me to imagine something being so tangled up that we wouldn't run a fence line given my experience working on that particular chore. Even so I was beginning to have an inkling of the location of the cemetery. There was a part of the farm that got real swampy and full of palmetto plants and sticker bushes and all sorts of other trees and brush. Granddaddy said there was a little rise several yards back that was right nice, but wasn't worth getting to because we couldn't do anything with it. He never said a word about a graveyard, probably because he knew I'd want to go look at it. The trees and brush were so thick I couldn't see anything that looked interesting, so I took his word for it.

"There's enough water in the creek right now that I could get you down there in a couple of flat bottom boats right quick like. It's an easy float from the put-in behind the little house." Peter pondered a little longer. We waited to hear him out. "Not sure we can use the Evinrudes."

"A trollin' motor might work. It'll kind of depend on how low the boats are riding."

"Nobody eat breakfast," Doc jumped in.

"Naw, that ought not make a difference." Peter mostly didn't follow when Doc was being silly. "Even if we have to row we could mostly float and tie up by the cemetery. We could just keep going after we're done. Pauline could meet us at the pull-in by the farm-to-market."

"Sure could. We'll just set a time, and I'll meet you there with the truck and trailer. We can just stack the boats on the trailer if the motors aren't connected up. Peter, you can just set up in them to hold them down. Y'all don't mind riding home in the back of the truck?"

Sister, Winnie, Susie B., and I were agreeable. Lee and Vera were less so, but they were good sports. Merril was the most enthusiastic of the whole bunch. "I've never done that and have always wanted to."

"I'll drive real slow," Pauline offered.

"Oh, please don't." Merril seemed giddy at the thought of it.

"All right, but I'll need to drive slow enough to keep Peter from bucking off."

"I'd 'preciate that," Peter said, dead serious. "We can go Tuesday. I'm taking some folks out on Lake Burton tomorrow, and there's church on Sunday. I purely promised Pauline I'd get some work done on the roof on Monday. Turns out we sprung a leak in that big rain."

"Oh dear, Peter. Did it make much of a mess?"

"No ma'am. It was located in a convenient place over the bathtub."

No one talked for a bit because we could see that Peter was still thinking about this trip. Interrupting his process would slow it down mightily. "We probably ought to take along a couple of .22s in case Speedy and I need to scare off some water moccasins."

I didn't know whether to be honored because Peter thought I'd be good at it or worried because, truth be known, I didn't want anything to do with a water moccasin. I also began worrying about what would happen if I scared one, and it headed over in my direction. I was even thinking I was a little grateful that Peter had said scare them off. I had no doubt that Peter could pick them off easy like, but he was saving me from teasing if I missed. All these thoughts were zooming around in my head, so I almost missed it when Pauline joined back in.

"You might ought to take something else along bigger than a .22. Haven't you spotted some wild pigs up that-a-way?"

"Sure 'nuff. I'll tote the hog-leg."

"What for, bait?" Vera asked.

"Vera, a hog-leg is a pistol—a big one," said Sister.

"My word. What are we getting ourselves into? Will Mutual of Omaha be accompanying us to film *Wild Kingdom*?"

"If they do, we're going to need more boats."

"Peter, she's exaggerating."

"I'm proud to hear it. I've done took some of them TV fellers on trips and they are mighty particular. They carry way too much stuff."

"How muddy is it down there?" Winnie asked a sensible question.

"Oh I'd be wearing me some muck boots."

"So how many of you have muck boots?" Me-Mama inquired.

"I'm not even sure what muck boots are," Vera said, "I feel as if I have spent the entire evening on another planet."

"Tall, waterproof boots that come up to about your knees."

Sister had some, I had some, and Merril had some. It turns out that Merril's people use them to get around in the snow. She'd brought them South with her at first because they were standard winter gear. She continued to bring them because they kept her feet dry even during the worst rainstorms. She'd thrown them in the car to come to Rowja "just in case."

Once Vera realized they were heavy duty snow boots, she knew she had a pair. "Sadly, they remain in the frozen tundra of the Midwest. They are not stylish in the least."

"I imagine among all of us we can rustle up enough pairs for everybody," Doc figured.

"We keep some extras at the store for folks Peter's guiding. They don't always have the right boots. Y'all are welcome to use them as long as you rinse them off."

"Now, Peter, we are going to pay you for leading this trip and getting the girls and Speedy there and back safe and sound," Me-Mama declared.

"No ma'am. All y'all's money is no good with us."

"That's right, Miz Esther. It's just part of our security service," Pauline added.

Now I don't exactly know how we got from "the cemetery wasn't worth visiting because all the graves were too old and half of them were in the water anyhow" to taking a fully-armed expedition, but that's where we were.

Taterhead Creek

On Saturday, everybody went their own way. We didn't get back together until Monday afternoon when we all met up at Me-Mama and Granddaddy's house to car pool over to Burtonville for the final game of the regular season.

Despite our poor practices, we beat the snot out of them. They would have called the game on account of the ten-run rule except that by the time we'd played the minimum number of innings, we were ahead of them by eighteen runs. Coach was doing everything he could think of to keep from running up the score. He even had me swinging away despite my talent for drawing walks. That's why I got my first extra base hit ever. Truth be told, it was just about my first hit ever.

What happened was, I swung as hard as I possibly could and smacked the ball into the outfield. This feat, in and of itself, surprised me and everybody on the bench and in the stands. The ball headed right between the centerfielder and the right fielder. Somehow or another they managed to run into each other. By the time one of the outfielders fetched the ball and threw it back, I was standing on third base, panting from having run so far so fast. The Altheans and Me-Mama and Granddaddy cheered so long and loud until I had to tip my cap. Smitty drove me in with another homer and gave me a big hug when I greeted her at the plate.

Our big game with the ringers from Hannibal would be in two weeks. Their county had more teams than we did, so it took them a week longer to get through their regular season. That was okay by us. Coach was giving us the week off to clear our heads and refocus. We'd begin serious practice Tuesday week.

We headed to the big house after the championship celebration at the Pizzazz. The game was the talk of the car ride back. Sister warned me not to get the "big head" and to be willing to go back to my strategy of walking; I wasn't Stan Musial yet. Coach had already made note of that.

Later in the evening, as everyone was heading for bed, we heard, "Oh no!" from the front room. Susie B. called out, "Can y'all come help me?"

We hurried to her room where she and Vera were lying flat on their stomachs looking under the chifferobe. "A tragedy has come upon Susie B."

"Vera, it looks like whatever happened to her happened to you as well."

"I wouldn't exactly call it a tragedy," said, Susie B., "but one of my earrings slipped out and rolled under the chifferobe."

Aunt Catherine's house was built at a time when folks didn't build closets. They had large pieces of furniture to use to store their clothes. The chifferobe in question was a monster. It was about eight foot tall and five foot across. Inside the double doors were two long shelves that ran all the way across the top. Under them on the left were drawers and on the right was an open area with a bar across the top for hang-up clothes. A deep drawer ran across the entire bottom. Some sort of carving covered the front. It sat on four wide, squatty feet, and it was topped by a decorated piece that Granddaddy called the tiara.

"Can anybody get your arm under it?" Lee Harris looked at me as the most likely candidate. I got down on my stomach and jammed my hand and arm as far under as I could. Try as I might, I could only get my arm in about halfway to my elbow. I couldn't reach the earring.

Susie B. grimaced. "I was hoping you could reach it. They aren't expensive, but they were a present, and I'd hate to lose one."

"Let's get a flashlight and a yardstick and see if we can knock it out," Winnie suggested. We retrieved the tools, and everybody took a turn trying to jar the earring free.

"I'm afraid all we're doing is making it worse. I think it's trapped in the gap between a couple of the floor boards. It might be in a knothole." Sister was lying on her side, looking up from the end of her second try. "It looks to me like we're going to have to move the chifferobe at least far enough so Speedy can reach under and pull it loose."

We looked at the chifferobe with dread. Vera gave it an exploratory shove. Nothing happened except Vera declaring something about the "labors of Hercules" and how the chifferobe was mocking us.

"The first thing we should do is empty it. There's probably seven hundred pounds of things in it," Sister said as she peered inside the double doors.

Winnie spoke up, "Probably not quite that much, but it's getting late, and we have an early call tomorrow. Susie B., do you need your earring for tomorrow's adventures?"

"Of course not."

"I'm thinking that we should just wait until we're back before trying to retrieve it. Goodness knows it's safe where it is."

We agreed that it was certainly safer than its partner and said our good nights for the evening.

Tuesday morning we had an early breakfast—for us. We determined that Granddaddy had run into Effie Floyd at church because she'd added information about our planned trip to the "mystery cemetery" to her write up about the trash fire. They were reading her column as the community news on the radio station. According to Miz Floyd's article, the party had been the social event of the summer.

At 8:00 we were headed down the driveway to Peter and Pauline's house. Lady was with us. She liked to go in a boat and helped discourage varmints. Buddy would remain at the big house where he could look handsome on the front porch. Sister thought, but was not certain, that the sight of a large dog might prevent another armadillo delivery.

Pauline was on the porch. "Oh good, Peter thought I might have to go roust y'all so as to leave on time. And you brought Lady. Peter's taking Tol and Pooch. The three of them will have a grand time."

Among Peter's considerable talents was dog training. People would dump dogs and puppies near Peter and Pauline's house or just flat out bring dogs and puppies to Peter. He could look at a dog and just know what he or she would be good for—sometimes it was for hunting, sometimes for herding. Peter would train them up to be some of the best dogs in the whole countryside.

Some dogs weren't suited for either hunting or herding. He'd teach them tricks and how to pose to emphasize what a cute pet they'd make. Pauline would sew outfits for the small dogs, so they'd look especially irresistible.

People would almost fight over a dog Peter had trained. He'd charge enough for them so he knew they wouldn't be used for fighting and then make the buyer sign a contract that they'd have the dog fixed or else he was allowed to take it back.

Every so often, though, a particularly smart dog would show up. You wouldn't know it to look at it, but Peter could see it right off. He would look every dog he got straight in the eye to figure out its talent. Once in a rare while, Peter would look at a dog and say, "That's my dog." Pauline allowed as to how once he said that, there was no convincing him otherwise. Peter said he could tell by the way the dog looked back at him that it would be a fine dog. Peter's dogs were inevitably girls. He said they were just smarter. Pauline never argued with that.

Pooch and Tol were two such dogs. Pooch was some sort of terrier/hound mix who had no idea how big she wasn't. She was black and tan, small, but with longish legs for her size. She could jump like crazy.

Pooch could stubborn her way through, over, under, or around most any obstacle and, once free, could run like nobody's business.

Tol, short for Tolerable Good Dog, was a lab/herding/pit bull mix, or so Peter thought, who was much calmer than Pooch unless motivated otherwise. Tol loved the water and loved to fetch. She also made sure that all of her people were accounted for at all times. Tol was mostly black with scattered pieces of fur in just about every color fur could be. Even though she would never win a beauty contest, she was sweet and fiercely protective of her people.

Peter figured it was a good idea to have dogs along "just in case." He didn't say just in case of what. He had already put a .22 in each of the boats and had the pistol strapped to his leg. Pauline had loaded a red wagon with some necessities for the trip—a couple of small coolers filled with Cokes and sandwich fixings and some grocery sacks with napkins, plates, plastic silverware, and toilet paper. She pulled it down to the small dock on Taterhead Creek, and we began unloading it into the two boats Peter had tied up. Vera was alarmed at the prospects of needing the toilet paper, but the rest of us took the notion of finding a bush in stride. Merril had never done that either.

As we were arranging everything in the boats, Pauline said, "Now let's go ahead and get y'all ready for skeeters. I've got Off and Skin So Soft. Who wants what?" It was a mixture of who wanted which product. Pauline added, "We'll check for ticks when y'all get back," as she distributed Good News gimme caps to those who didn't have a hat. "No sense in burning to a crisp."

Peter, Susie B., Lee Harris, Vera and Tol were going to be taking the first boat. Sister, Winnie, Merril, Pooch, Lady, and I would follow. Peter and Sister sat in the back to run the trolling motors. Peter said, "Tol, get in the front and watch for low places and snags." We guessed Peter was serious about that. He didn't kid around much. Tol jumped in the first boat, put her paws on the front edge, and looked down at the water. Every so often once we got going, she'd bark. Peter would slow down, stretch up, look down the creek, and adjust the course. I was in the front of our boat and would signal Sister on how to follow Peter's course.

Taterhead Creek wound around a lot, and there were a lot of things in it. It was almost impossible to see very deep into the reddish brown water. Even so, the trip was really pretty. The creek was running deep enough and was smooth as a bathtub except for the occasional ripple where a bug or fish, or heaven forbid, snake, would move. The trees formed an archway across the narrowest parts. It was like floating through a long, green tunnel. Squirrels chattered and mockingbirds scolded as we passed by. Sometimes the banks were about level with the creek, other times they were way up over our heads where the water had cut through a hillside during hard rains over the years. The electric motors made almost no sound. Everybody was pretty quiet, lost in their thoughts about what we might find.

We were running slow so as not to get hung up on anything. Peter didn't seem completely confident in how much lead time he'd get from Tol. Long about 10 o'clock, Peter called back, "This here's the old bridge. We'll put in around the next bend. Go ahead and cut your motor."

Sure enough, we could see what was left of some rotting bridge supports on either side of the creek. If we combined what we could see with what we could imagine, we could figure out where the old road had been. We knew the property to our right belonged to our family. We weren't sure about the other side.

We rounded the bend. Peter was already out of his boat, standing in the shallows. He was holding the line to his boat and called for me to chunk him our line. I am happy to say that I performed that task to his satisfaction. He pulled our boat over and put out his arm to help me jump out. I held our boat while he drug his boat up as close as he could to the solid ground and tied it off to a thick root sticking out of where the hill had washed away. Over the years, a small beach had formed in front of about a six or seven foot wall of clay. Brush was piled at either side. When Peter finished securing his boat, he pulled the other boat in next to the first. The Altheans and dogs jumped out onto the narrow strip of reddish clay and sand that had washed downstream.

Looking around, I noticed pieces of tombstones lying around the beach and hanging on the top of the hill. It was hard to see them amid all the brush, but the more I looked the more I could see. If I didn't know they were there, I'd never have noticed them.

Peter put his hands on his hips looked around and said, "We gotta figure out how to get from down here to up there."

"While you work on that, I'm going to check these stones to see if any say Tom," Winnie was already at work looking at the stones on the beach, "I hope not because they are very worn and some are upside down."

Peter poked around in the brush a while longer and said, "While I'm figuring this out we could go ahead and unload the boats." Sister hopped back in one boat and then the other to pass out the coolers and other supplies. "Peter, do you want the rifles?"

"Yep, and look under the seats. There's some blankets for us to sit on for the picnic. Be careful. I done wrapped machetes, clippers, and limb loppers up in 'em. Git them, too. Looks like we'll need 'em."

"Will do. Oh, here's a first aid kit. Want it, too?"

"I reckon. If we get it out, we won't need it."

The beach began to get crowded. I wasn't quite sure how everything that was on the beach had fit in the boat. The Altheans were about finished with the second boat when Peter said, "Speedy, come over here." I did, and the next thing I knew Peter had picked me up and tossed me up on the hill with the graveyard.

"Call Lady and Tol," Peter ordered.

"Lady, girl. Tol, come see me! Here girls, c'mon."

Lady and Tol worried themselves back and forth across the beach as I called. Pooch took to bouncing straight up and down as though she could pogo herself up here. Finally, Lady spotted a passable way and started bulling herself through the brush, uncovering a gentle slope as she went. Tol was close behind. The two of them managed to push down enough brush that Peter could come along and whack at the worst of it. The Altheans followed behind stomping down the stumps and briers as they brought up the supplies.

Peter got to the top and checked Tol and Lady, who were very pleased with themselves, for cuts and scrapes. He pronounced them sound and offered them treats from the bag he kept in his coverall pocket.

We took a little time to get our bearings. The cemetery itself was in a fairly clear space. It was grown up some with brush and some sticker bushes, but we could mostly see at least the tops of the tombstones now that we were up here. We could also spot bits and pieces of an iron fence that had surrounded the cemetery at one point. Outside the fence, the brush got thicker as the hill dropped off into a swampy area. We were standing behind the area Granddaddy wouldn't fence. The big house was maybe a mile or two away, but it might as well have been on the moon.

"We should get to work," Winnie pointed out. "We want to be through in time to meet Pauline at 3:30, and it's nearly eleven now." It had taken a good while to get unloaded and up here.

We started working. This was a whole different prospect. We were used to fanning out along pretty neat rows and covering a lot of ground at once. Here, though, we had to find a tombstone, chop away at the brush, and then try to read what it said. We decided to work our way around the side to the back and then across to the other side. We were thankful that it was a tiny cemetery. To add to the problem, we had to get the information from all the stones. Some of the tombstones had long essays on them with Bible verses and all sorts of what Sister called "philosophical ramblings."

"I swear, Melanie, your people certainly were serious," Lee Harris pointed out after reading one particularly gloomy sentiment about the cruelty of the world.

"Judging from these dates, they must have been dropping like flies."

"Your grandmother's right though. These stones are all from way before 1916."

"Even so, they're really helpful in completing our history," said Susie B., ever the optimist.

"That's true. I wonder if we can figure out what killed them—yellow fever maybe?"

Until that time, the dogs had been alternatively playing and sleeping in the shade. Right that minute Tol and Lady were sleeping. Pooch was digging a hole ignoring Vera's orders to stay away from bones. All of a sudden, Pooch jerked her head up out of the hole. Her hackles went up, and she turned back toward the creek and growled.

This got everybody's attention, especially Tol and Lady who jumped up and commenced to barking. We were almost to the far side of the cemetery away from the creek, so we couldn't see anything. Before we could say anything, we heard cussing coming from down by the boats. Lady and Tol tore down the path we'd broken, and Pooch just launched herself off the edge of the cliff. Peter yelled, "Who's down there?" pulled the pistol from the holster, and headed back toward the creek. Sister was right behind him. She grabbed one of the .22s on her way. Vera was screaming, "Pirates! Pirates?" The rest of us followed Peter and Sister. The footing was treacherous, so we couldn't make much headway.

By the time we made it to the path, there wasn't much to see. Tol was swimming back to the beach. Lady was holding some blue material. Pooch was barking and bouncing two or three feet in the air. The boats were gone. Peter and Sister were trudging up the path. About then, we heard someone holler from around the downstream bend, "Go home!"

Sister spun in that direction, eyes blazing, "I am home, you sorry jackass!"

"If that don't beat all." Peter was as close to being mad as I'd ever seen. "I wish I'd laid eyes on those—well, I just wish I had. C'mon, dogs."

Sister was so mad she couldn't even talk. The rest of us were in shock until Lady came up and we saw that she was holding a chunk of blue jeans and some underwear with red hearts on them. "Lady, girl, at least you did some good," Peter laughed.

"And I hope she got her pound of flesh."

Peter poured some of the melted ice into a bowl he'd brought. The dogs drank hard. "What should we do?" Lee Harris asked.

"I guess we're going to have to either hack our way through the brush or wait until Pauline goes to meet us, and we're not there."

"I hate to scare her like that, but I don't know if we could cut our way through and get to the house before she left to come get us."

We could tell Peter was thinking. "Can I borry a sheet of paper?"

"Of course."

"Sister, will you write Pauline a note that tells her that we're stuck here and ask her to come down the creek with a couple of boats."

"Yes, but . . ."

"And ask her to call Doc to meet us at the boat ramp on the farm-to-market."

Sister was writing all of this on a sheet torn from her composition book. When she was done, she handed it to Peter. He folded it and put in a baggie that had been filled with some Fritos we'd already eaten. He rolled up the baggie into a tight cylinder. He called Pooch over and took off her collar. He got some tape out of the first aid kit and secured the cylinder under Pooch's collar by wrapping the tape all the way around it and the collar.

"Do you mind writing Pauline's name on this here tape? Write it big as you can."

Sister did so. Peter put Pooch's collar back around her neck, stood up, and said, "Pooch, where's Pauline?" Pooch jerked her head up, looked around to get her bearings, and whimpered. Peter asked again, "Pooch, where's Pauline?" Pooch stood there a second more and quivered a little. "Pooch, go get her." With that Pooch took off like a shot through the brush headed in the direction of the big house.

Peter looked after her and said, "I reckon she'll get there before we could. It's not all that far as the crow flies. If she makes it in time, it'll save Pauline a lot of worry. If she doesn't, we're no worse off that we were before. Pooch will just wait on the porch for her to get back."

"Will Pooch be okay?" I was worried.

"I 'spect so." I could tell Peter was worried from the way he was staring into the brush, but he wasn't going to let on.

"We might as well have our picnic and then get back to work. There's nothing else we can do," Winnie pointed out.

"All right, but Speedy, I want you and Lady to get over by the drop off in case those fellers come back. Take the .22. Don't shoot at them, but shoot near enough to them so they'll know we mean business."

I wasn't too keen on this idea, but did as Sister said. I could barely taste my sandwich.

It was between 2:30 and 3:00. I was still standing guard when I heard Sister call, "Y'all? Y'all? Y'ALL? Come here. Help me, quick!" True to herself, she had wandered over to a part of the cemetery that was a ways off from where they'd been finding tombstones. She was chopping frantically at a mound of brush. From where I was it looked like she was after bees or fire ants. "Y'all, come quick," she hollered again. I left my post and scrambled through the brush to join the others. Sister had cut away at enough of the brush to read,

TOMMY ROY CROFT
D. 1916

We stood spellbound as she hacked away and uncovered,

AN ANGEL FELL TO EARTH

Lee Harris gasped, "Oh my God. Tom is real."

"And he's my uncle," Merril added tonelessly.

Rescue

We stood for a while staring at the tombstone until just about everybody started talking at once. That wasn't getting us anywhere, so Winnie shushed us and tried to get the discussion more organized. We all agreed that we had found Tom, but were perplexed as to how Merril had decided he was her uncle.

"Is it because MiMi said his name was Roy?"

"You can't be positive since the name here isn't Reynolds."

"Didn't your uncle take a train out of the county?"

Merril continued staring at the tombstone. "No, it's him. I'm sure." Tears were welling up in her eyes.

"How do you know for sure?"

"Roycroft is the name of the craft guild in East Aurora." At that, we fell silent. Several folks started sniffing back tears–me included.

After a bit, Winnie cleared her throat. "Y'all, we only have a few more to go. We might as well finish up. We can talk about this while we work. Our job's not done."

She was right. Sister sent me back to my post. I leaned against a headstone that seemed stable. Lady and Tol came over to have their ears scratched. They knew something was worrisome.

The Altheans and Peter continued working and speculating about Tom. They were wondering all sorts of things—mainly how he died, why nobody knew he died, and how he got in our family cemetery. They were mostly avoiding the main questions—was he really murdered and how had he let us know he was there.

The heat and the work and winding down from the excitement of finding Tom must have gotten to me. I wasn't doing anything but sitting by a tombstone petting dogs, so I kept feeling myself nodding off. I was drifting away again when Lady and Tol both sat up. My head had been resting on Lady, so when she sat up, I banged it on the tombstone. I was about to fuss at her when I heard what they'd heard. Up Taterhead Creek around the bend, I could hear barking. "Y'all, it's Pooch. She's back!"

Sure enough, the next thing I knew, Pauline came up in a boat. Pooch was standing in the front, barking. The other dogs scampered down to meet her. Pauline was towing another boat behind her. Peter met her at the beach and tied off the boats. "You're the purtiest girl I ever seen." Pooch thought he was talking to her, but I believe he was talking to Pauline.

"I'd have been here sooner, but Pooch was so excited that I had a hard time getting her to stop bouncing long enough to get her collar off. I've never seen a dog drink so much."

We were all telling Pooch what a good girl she was even though she already knew it. "I told her she didn't have to ride back with me, but she insisted. It was slow going because the towed boat wouldn't necessarily go where I wanted it to."

We all allowed to how we'd lost track of time after we found Tom. Pauline was interested in seeing the grave. We took her over to the side where he was. "Way over here all by hisself. Ain't that something?" Peter told her.

"Well, no wonder he wanted to be found," Pauline pointed out, "but we probably need to head on. Doc is going to meet us at the pull-in not too long from now. He was mighty concerned, and I didn't know what to tell him other than y'all had headed off in two boats, and now you were stuck, and I needed to get you two more boats."

"I bet that did worry him."

We packed everything in the boats best we could. It was surprising how much less room there was even though Pauline wasn't very big. We finally got everything loaded, and Peter pushed both boats off from the beach and into deeper water. He clamored into the back of the second one, started the motor, and we headed off.

We wound around a few more bends in Taterhead Creek, maybe a quarter or half mile or so, when Vera shouted from the lead boat, "Ahoy, mateys. Boats, ho!" Then Pauline called back, "Peter, it's our boats."

Sure as shootin', we came around the bend, and there were Peter's boats snagged in the root ball of a tree that had tumped on the side of the creek.

"Them boys must not be as good as Pauline at navigating the creek," Peter noted.

Sister added, "They must not even be as good as Tol." We all had to laugh at that.

"Speedy, tie us on to that there limb, and let me see if I can get them free." Peter hopped from our boat into one of the other boats. He hollered over to Pauline, "Y'all can go on ahead."

"I'm not going anywhere until all my chickens are home to roost."

"All right, then."

Peter worked for a while until he said, "I got both of 'em to come a-loose. Sister, you run the boat I was in. Speedy, hop over here, and you take this one."

"Are you sure?" I had never taken charge of a boat without supervision.

"You'll be good. You've run a boat before. Jump on over here." I scrambled over and landed face first in the bottom of the boat.

"Not an auspicious start," Vera declared.

"Pauline, you go first. Sister, you follow Pauline," Peter ordered. To me, more quietly he said, "Don't worry about getting snagged. The creek opens up right around the bend, the water's deep, but the current's not too strong. Just follow your Sister." Then loud again, he called, "Tol, come over here and keep Speedy company."

Tol took the opportunity to get in the water again. She jumped out of Pauline's boat and paddled over. Peter reached over the side and lifted Tol into the boat. Toll shook off all over us and took her place in the front. "Tol'll let you know if there's any trouble. If she barks, cut the motor and lift it up. You'll get right on over whatever it might be." With that, Peter jumped into the fourth boat. It rocked precariously, but before long he had it balanced. "Let's get ourselves on out of here 'fore anything else happens."

True to what Peter said, the tree line dropped off right around the next bend. Taterhead Creek was wider and deeper. We started making good time because we didn't have to look for hazards through the thick, muddy water. It wasn't long before we saw the farm-to-market bridge and our reception committee at the boat ramp. It was the first ramp on the creek because Taterhead Creek was consistently deep enough at that point to launch a boat reliably. A lot of people put in there to get to the lake or to go up a ways and fish among the brushy places.

Granddaddy was there with Peter's truck and boat trailer. There was another truck and trailer backed down to the water. "I asked Parker to meet us here. Pauline said something about four boats, and I just couldn't see stacking four boats on the back of one trailer."

In addition, Me-Mama was there in the Imperial. She had driven Granddaddy out to Peter's to pick up the truck and trailer and had decided that all of us and all our stuff couldn't fit in the trucks. MiMi had come along for the ride.

We pulled the boats out of the water and disconnected the motors. Once the motors were off the back and the equipment was unloaded, the boats didn't weigh very much and were easy to stack on the trailers. We put the motors and all the stuff that wouldn't blow out back in the boats. Next, we divided up who was going to ride where. Pauline drove Peter's truck. The dogs rode up front with her because they didn't have any way to hold on in the back, and Peter didn't want them to get hurt.

"Clearly, we are expendable," Vera declared. No one paid her much attention.

Granddaddy rode with Uncle Parker, and Vera, Susie B., and Lee Harris climbed in the Imperial. The rest of us rode in the backs of the trucks. Merril got her wish and rejoiced in the wind blowing through her hair as we drove to Peter and Pauline's house. Upon arriving, we unhooked the trailers. Uncle Parker said he'd leave his so we wouldn't have to rush to get it unloaded.

Me-Mama popped the trunk on the Imperial. They had stopped by the Q-Stick and gotten brisket sandwiches and fixings. She also had a cooler of Cokes and Big Reds. We ate sitting on Peter and Pauline's porch and steps and told them about the day. Vera had several questions about piracy laws in Texas. No one knew the answer to any of them.

We were all about done in as we trudged down the driveway to the big house. "We're going to have to time these showers carefully if we're to have a chance at warm water."

"I do feel a little stronger having eaten."

"At some point, not now, we're going to have to figure out what to do about this paper. It's due the 30th."

"This Monday?"

"Speedy, you don't have a game that day, right?"

"Coach gave us the week off. We'll start practicing for sure again next Tuesday."

"I'm so sorry I'll miss the game with Hannibal, but my plane ticket to New York is next week. I wish I could stay and watch." Merril looked genuinely unhappy.

"That's okay. If we win, I'll send you the newspaper write-up in a letter."

"And if you lose?" Vera smiled and cocked her head.

"We'll get 'em next year."

We managed to get showers without anybody freezing and turned in early.

Poodle

Right off the bat Wednesday morning, we could tell that Winnie had spent part of the night not sleeping. She'd been organizing the day and the rest of the week. "I suggest we rescue the earring before we start finishing up this project. I don't want us to forget about it or get distracted," she announced at the breakfast table.

She had a point. A couple of us had already forgotten about it what with Tom and all. "You're probably right. We'll get on it after breakfast."

We had a long breakfast, talking a lot about Tom, but finally went up to face the chifferobe. First, we began pulling everything out. Winnie cautioned that we should keep things in order, so we'd know how to put it all back. Lee Harris and Merril put themselves in charge of organizing. The rest of us arranged ourselves into a bucket brigade as Sister pulled things out. She'd call out when she changed location. We agreed that we'd pay more attention to the treasures held by the chifferobe as we put them back. We promised Winnie that we would not become obsessed with what we found.

Once we got it empty, it was time to move the chifferobe. We decided it was probably best to pivot it on two legs until we could reach the earring. We decided not to try to move the whole thing. "I'm afraid the tiara makes it top-heavy, and we don't want it to come over on us," said Sister.

"We need to lift it on this side though to keep from scratching up the floor too bad," I added.

We discussed strategy for a while before making our first attempt. It did not go well. "Whoa! Whoa! Whoa!" After two more equally unsuccessful attempts, Sister said, "We need somebody tall. Speedy, go see if Peter is down there."

He was. He'd already unloaded the boat trailers and delivered Uncle Parker's back to him. Peter was fine with coming up to help move the chifferobe. Pauline was, too. She'd always wanted to know what was in it. We went back to the big house.

Vera pressed the back of her hand to her forehead. "Alas, Peter and Pauline, we call upon your assistance once more."

Peter looked at the chifferobe for a bit until they came to an agreement. He arranged us where we should be and told us who should pull, who should lift, who should push, and who should balance.

Then, "1 . . . 2 . . . 3 . . . go!"

The chifferobe moved in a lurch. I was on the back corner, on the pivot side holding for balance. About the time, Lee Harris exclaimed, "There it is. Got it!" I heard something slide across the top of the tilted chifferobe. I looked up just in time to see something teetering on the edge. I knew I couldn't let go, so I ducked and held on as it fell off and hit me on the head.

"Ow!"

"Speedy, are you all right?"

"Something fell off the chifferobe and hit me on the head."

"Let's get it swung back, and then we'll assess the damage." We maneuvered the chifferobe back in place.

"You're not bleeding. Is that what hit you?" It was a packet of letters tied up in ribbons.

"I guess so."

"Now, these are interesting," said Sister.

Peter did not seem to agree. "Y'all got anything else you need me for?"

"No, Peter, thank you."

Sister had pulled off the ribbon and was looking at the letters. "These all seem to be to Aunt Catherine from Uncle Poodle." She flipped though the envelopes. "Some are from France, I guess during World War I. Some of these others are from random small towns in Texas, Oklahoma, and Louisiana. I suppose they were minor league towns. Look, here's one from Chicago and one from New York. There's a few from St. Louis."

"He played for the Browns," I noted.

"Oh, let's read them."

"Now, we agreed we wouldn't get obsessed with whatever we found in the chifferobe."

"Oh, Winnie, how can we not?"

Winnie knew that she would lose this particular round. She said, "Let's at least divide them and just talk about the best parts. And, by best parts, I mean things that are really cool and/or things that might have some marginal connection to this project."

"Deal."

Winnie continued, "Maybe later this summer we could type them up and send everyone copies." Winnie was probably hoping this offer would speed today's reading.

Sister put the letters in the order of their postmarks and dealt them out. We each had a small stack of letters. Some of the letters were only a page or so. Others were several pages thick.

"He had nice penmanship," noted Vera.

"And remarkably good grammar," added Winnie.

"He went to college for a while," I said.

"Speedy, how do you know all this?"

Before I could answer, Sister said, "Oh, Speedy is an expert on all things Poodle."

We read for a little while. Every so often someone would call out a passage from a letter that was particularly funny. Pauline found a story about how Poodle getting the mumps had kept his whole unit from having to go to the front. Poodle claimed he deserved a medal for saving so many lives.

We were reading along when I heard Sister say quietly, "Oh no." I looked over. Sister was crying. Sister hardly ever cried except when one of the animals got hurt or died.

"What is it?"

Sister tried to compose herself. "This is terrible."

"Did Poodle die?"

"No."

"Can you read it to us?"

"Yes, no, I guess. I'll have to read the whole thing."

"Do you want me to read it?"

"No. Just give me a second. I have to let it settle in." Winnie found a box of Kleenex and handed her a couple. Sister blew her nose, took a deep breath, and blew it out slowly.

"It's from St. Louis. *My dearest Catherine.*"

"I love the sweet way he starts his letters."

"*My dearest Catherine. I owe you an explanation for why we can't be together as often as we'd like.*"

"Did Poodle have an affair?"

"A secret family?"

"No. It's worse than that. He goes on. *I'm going to tell you a story, but you have to promise never to tell it to anybody—your very lives could be in danger.*"

"What?"

Sister nodded and continued, "*Everybody else on our side who knows the story is gone except for me, but folks from the other side are still around, and they would come after you if they found out anyone knew their secret. I've been carrying this with me for many years now, and I must tell somebody. Every time I come back to the home place, the guilt I feel just about kills me. Drinking helps a bit. I need to stay away from that place, but I want to be with you. I know you*" *can't leave home. My life on the road is no place for you, but you have to know why I can't stay there. Promise me you'll burn this letter. It can never get out, and they must never know what I know."*

The room grew silent and smaller as we listened to Sister read.

"One night your Papa and I were out on the back steps having a smoke and a snort and talking about the world's problems. It was late, and everyone was in bed. We noticed a glow toward the back of the property, and we headed that way to make sure nothing had caught fire. We walked past the old fever cemetery and started to smell smoke. We could tell it wasn't on our property but needed to check to be sure that somebody knew about it, and it wouldn't jump the creek. Not long after we crossed the old bridge, we came up on the most terrible thing I ever saw, even in the war.

We were cowards and hid in the brush. Some of those Harris boys and that passel they ran around with were there with old Captain Thornton from the war. They had built a fire and were beating and kicking some poor fellow to death. There wasn't any point in going to find the law because the law, that Deputy Austin, was among them. We figured out from all their hollering and hoorahing that it was that Yankee boy they were killing.

Catherine, honey, they even had a couple of children with them. Old Captain Thornton had brought along that son he had by his second or third wife, the one that married him for his pension. He's that boy that turned to be a preacher. That little Harris girl that follows John Bell around was screaming at them to stop hurting her angel. I'm so ashamed we didn't do anything, but they would have lit into us. They was fully out for blood.

Finally, one of them went and fetched the boy's horse and hoisted him up on it. I think and I pray that he might have already been dead. They had to hold him up to put the rope around his neck. They tied the other end up in the tree. One of them Harris boys walked over to the fire and pulled out a glowing stick. He blew on it, waved it in front of the girl, and said 'Let's see your angel fly.' He touched the stick to the horse's rump and it took off. One of them hollered, 'That'll keep you away from our girls.' That Yankee-boy was just hanging there."

"Oh Merril, I'm so sorry," Lee Harris said through her tears.

"I know it wasn't you. You're not a part of them," Merril replied, "Poor Bertie. At least somebody cared for him." She reached out and held Lee Harris's hand.

"There's more."

"They hoorahed some more and looked for the horse. They couldn't find it and got into a row over it. They were still fussing and punching as they rode off down the road.

We waited until we knew they were gone and went and cut him down. It was that Yankee boy all right. We carried him back across the bridge to the fever cemetery. Your papa said that they were going to leave him to the animals and the least we could do was bury him.

Your papa left me with him in the cemetery while he went to get some help. While he was gone, I looked through the boy's clothes to see if I could find anything that would let us be able to get word to his family. I found a little money, some playing cards, and a folded up letter to 'Tommy' that was signed 'your loving mother.' Soon enough, your papa came back with Toots and his two oldest boys."

Sister interjected here, "Toots is Doc's daddy. Don't ask."

"With Toots and his two oldest boys and a couple of old quilts. Toots and the boys had sod busters and shovels. We dug a grave off to the side and wrapped the boy in the quilts, laid him in and covered him up. We buried him with the letter and cards and took the money to the church. When we were throwing on the last few shovelfuls, we heard some nickering off behind us. The boy's horse had come back looking for him. Toots caught hold of him and led him over to see what we'd done.

Catherine, I swear that horse snuffed the ground and kicked at it. Toots said he'd doctor on the burnt place, and he and your Papa headed back toward the barn, but not before we all swore a solemn oath that we'd not speak of what we'd seen or done.

But that wasn't the end of it. The guilt was eating at your Papa something fierce. He had implied that he'd bought the horse when the fellow had left town. The Harris boys and their crew knew better, but they probably figured that the horse had just wandered up, and we had took it in. The story started going around the county that the boy had sold it when he went off to fight the Kaiser. Your papa didn't contradict them. All the girls declared the boy to be a hero. They called him Roy Croft, but we knew his mama called him Tommy.

One day your papa announced that he had big farm business and had me carry him to Mayhaw to catch the train to Dallas. I picked him up the next day, and he told me what he'd done. A few weeks later, he and I took the wagon up to Hannibal. He didn't want word to get out in Mayhaw. The train men loaded the wagon with the headstone your papa had bought. Toots and his boys met us in the cemetery, and we set it up at the grave. They'd already been at work knocking down the bridge. Your papa wanted anyone who might take a notion to come over to our side to have to work to do it.

We helped them finish with the bridge. We didn't plan this, but the rubble mostly dammed off Taterhead Creek. The creek come way up the next big rain and because it couldn't go much of anywhere it flooded the low places around the cemetery hill and cut it off. Your papa let it be known that it must have been a beaver dam that caused the flood that washed out the bridge. He said the land back there wasn't worth what it would cost to set things right. No one questioned him.

There you have it, Catherine. I hate for you to share this burden, but I can no longer bear it alone. I hope you can understand better why I'm so nervous when I'm there. We must not let this secret get out. The meanness runs deep across the creek. Please be silent and be safe. I will return at season's end, and we can go away for a long visit.

Your ever faithful, Poodle"

Finishing Up

A lot happened in the days after Sister read Poodle's letter. Sister declared that we weren't going to keep Tom's murder a secret anymore, and we went about telling everybody we could think of about it. We told the rest of our families, and Merril called her folks in East Aurora to fill them in. Doc called Effie Floyd, who planned on writing an historical expose. Winnie got in touch with Dr. Byrd to relay what we'd learned and to ask for advice on how to handle the project.

Dr. Byrd recommended that the mystery and the search for Tom take center stage. She encouraged the Altheans to take creative license because she thought telling Tom's story would make for a project like none before. The Altheans began the process of forming their notes and recollections into the final paper. My services were no longer required.

I was still busy. Granddaddy had come up with a project for him, me, Peter, and some of the cousins. We worked on it the rest of the week. He and Me-Mama and Pauline also came up with plans that involved all of us, but would be a surprise for the Altheans. It was good that Coach had called off practice that week because it would have been hard to work into the schedule Doc had set.

I still spent evenings at the big house where I'd learn things about how the paper was going. I'd overhear snippets of information they were considering. Here's some of what I gathered.

One night, Lee Harris informed everyone that her uncle had gone out to the family compound and had confronted the descendants of Jefferson Davis and John Bell. As it turns out, they were the cause of much of the mischief we had experienced. It seemed that the tale of the Damnyankee had been handed down as a secret source of family pride. They had protected the womenfolk of the county from the scurrilous invader from the north. Effie Floyd's article had alerted them to our search. They took to sneaking around trying to figure out our plans. They were the mysterious visitors who left the gate open, they had delivered the armadillo to the mailbox, and they had made off with the boats. All of it was an attempt to discourage us or to scare us into dropping our search. Lee Harris's uncle even found out about some things they'd done that we hadn't even noticed. Vera chalked their efforts up to "raging incompetence."

Word came to us that Effie Floyd had done some thinking about her own family. She recalled that her brothers had been running buddies with the Harris boys. She decided that her missing newspapers coincided roughly with the time that Tommy Reynolds was in the county. She figured that at some point her brothers decided to remove all traces of or references to Roy Croft in case anybody came looking for him. So, they took all the newspapers from that period just to be safe. Miz Floyd offered to fund the Altheans on a trip to the state archives in Austin to locate and retrieve copies of her missing newspapers. They were seriously considering it.

The Reverend Thornton's radio sermon focused on the Ten Commandments, especially the one about not bearing false witness. Winnie snapped off the radio before he could get too far. Before she did, we learned that the Altheans were a part of the "academic and Hollywood communities" and thus nothing any of them said was to be trusted. Vera was thrilled to be considered a part of the Hollywood community and strutted around the big house declaring that she was "ready for her close up."

Every so often, the project would bog down as they discussed how everything that had gone on would fit together. They had no clue how to explain the ways in which Tom had contacted us.

"Maybe he's been waiting all this time for the right configuration of people."

"That could be. It took Lee Harris and Merril both being in the same room to get him started."

"And he only wanted to talk to them with the Ouija Board."

"Plus we had some of Papa and Toots' people. It was a complete mix."

"Write it down."

They wondered if they should draw a connection among Tom, Tommy Austin, and Thomas Jackson, Trey, the boy whose funeral Doc had mistakenly attended.

"Bertie said the sins of the fathers are visited upon the sons, and she was right about angels falling from the sky."

"And Aunt Jewel said he calmed down when she came down the hall and saw him."

"You don't think she saw him, do you?"

"At this point, I wouldn't bet against it."

"Back to the subject. Are we going to claim that Tom, Tommy, and Trey are somehow tied together through time?" Winnie asked.

"You think Tom was seeking revenge?"

"Or there's some karmic retribution?"

"I just don't know."

"Maybe it's like MiMi said," Sister offered.

"Whatever do you mean?"

"Well, before y'all got here she warned me and Speedy that people die in threes, and that's three Toms."

They also considered what Tom asked of them.

"We've found him, so there's that."

"And we've let people know about him and his story, so we've taken care of that request."

"He also wants to go home."

"I know, but it's been a long time, and he was only wrapped up in quilts, there . . ." Sister's voice trailed off.

"It's fine," Merril said, "I'll take his memory back with me, and we'll have a family remembrance when I get home. That should suffice."

Mostly, though, they wrote, edited, typed, and answered the phone. Sister muttered about how the well-wishers were going to drive them all crazy. They'd gotten a little bit of a reprieve when Dr. Byrd called on Thursday to say that she'd like to visit the big house and maybe go see Tom's grave. The Altheans told her that the big house was completely doable, but that Tom's grave could be a problem. Dr. Byrd agreed and said that she'd be here Monday. She offered to take the paper back with her. That meant the Altheans wouldn't have to scramble to get it to the post office by noon on Saturday.

While they were working on their project, we were working on ours.

Saturday afternoon, Doc, Me-Mama, and MiMi drove up in the Imperial. The Altheans were hard at work, grateful that they hadn't had to stay up all night to get the paper in the mail.

"Are y'all about finished?" Doc asked.

"Melanie is typing the last few pages, and we're all taking turns proofreading."

"That's wise," Me-Mama noted. "The more eyes the better."

"Girls, we have a surprise for you," Doc announced. I smiled because I'd been working all week on the surprise.

"We all done cleaned up the cemetery."

Jaws dropped.

"Yep, Peter has bush-hogged through to the cemetery and hauled in gravel to make a pathway."

Sister saw the question coming and headed it off. "Vera, it's like a lawn mower with superpowers."

Granddaddy just shook his head. "Speedy and some cousins cleared away the brush and trash. Peter took a few pick-up loads over to the trash pile. I'm guessing we'll be able to have another fire soon."

"We could no longer abide such neglect."

"MiMi, please remember that we'd all forgotten about it just like Papa wanted us to do."

"And besides, they aren't your people."

"Nonetheless, they should be treated with more respect."

"Anyhow, it's a clean way to get back there."

"I am not surprised that Speedy could engage in such deception, but Peter?" Vera was flabbergasted.

"What do you mean?"

"One day we asked him about all the noise and activity back there, and he said that some of the trees had pine beetles, and y'all were cutting them out before they ate everything in sight. He said it with such a straight face," Susie B. explained.

"I admit we had to practice it, and Pauline had to convince him that we'd tell y'all the truth soon enough. She connected it up to Santa Claus and the Easter Bunny."

I was about to bust. "Can I tell them about tomorrow?"

"Yes, Speedy."

I talked fast before somebody could interrupt me. "Tomorrow after church and dinner, we're going down there with Mama's metal detector and see if we can find anything around Tom's grave. Maybe Poodle didn't find all the coins or something."

Me-Mama added, "It will ease Papa and Poodle and those who helped them."

"Mama has always wanted to use her metal detector," Sister sighed. "McRiley's is closed Sundays, so here's her chance."

Merril began crying and said, "Thank you."

Granddaddy sniffed a little, cleared his throat and said, "If we find anything or not, either way on Monday we're going to have a service for Tom at Woodrock. Your Dr. Byrd is coming down for it, too. She was happy to be invited."

"That explains her flexibility in taking the paper."

After talking a while more, the three of them drove off in the Imperial leaving the Altheans to finish the project.

Sunday afternoon was sunny and clear. It was not humid. The whole bunch of us made our way down the path Peter had carved through the brush. The cemetery was neat and tidy. I looked around with pride as the Altheans oohed and aahed. Me and my cousins had cut back all the brush and scrubbed the tombstones. We had even gotten as much of the iron fence up as was left. We'd set the tombstones up and gotten all the parts of the broken ones next to each other. Peter said we'd haul up the ones down in the creek as soon as the water went down.

"Doc, was all this your idea?" Merril asked softly.

For once, he didn't say anything. He just cast his eyes down and nodded.

Mama headed over to Tom's grave and turned on the metal detector. It made the usual spaceship noises. She began sweeping it back and forth and up and down. Every now and then, she'd stop and turn a few dials to adjust its sensitivity. It was hard for us to breathe. This went on for what seemed to be forever until suddenly she exclaimed, "There's something here!" She seemed as surprised as anybody.

Peter went over and took shovels and sod busters out from under the tarp where we'd been storing our tools all week. Mama indicated where we should dig, and we took after it. We even let Pooch help. She was quite enthusiastic, so much so that Peter eventually had to call her off. We'd dig a while, and then Mama would go over the area to see if we'd missed what she'd seen. "I hope it's not a tin can or a pop top. I find lots of those."

The deeper we got the slower we went. Winnie and the other Altheans started sifting through the dirt we'd moved. Peter was about to pull up another shovelful when I saw something shiny, "Peter, what's that?"

Mama jumped in the hole, picked it up, rubbed on it, and declared, "It's a button. A brass button. This is accelerating."

Sister translated, "Exhilarating, I think."

Work slowed to a crawl. The Altheans were combing through the dirt shovelful by shovelful. Finally, Mama pronounced that nothing else was showing up on the metal detector. Then she checked the dirt that had been thrown to the side just to be sure we hadn't missed anything. Nothing showed up there either. All in all, we had three brass buttons, a belt buckle, and a fifty cent piece dated 1912. Nothing else.

We held Tom's service Monday morning at 10:00. Peter built a small box to hold the things we'd found. Pauline had printed the name Tom Reynolds and the words "an angel" on the top. Peter made it permanent with his wood burner. Pauline sewed a drawstring bag out of gold drapery material to put the box in. That way Merril could carry it on the plane without too much curiosity directed her way.

There was quite a turnout for the service. All of the families and friends who had helped us were there. Daddy had closed McRiley's due to a "death in the family" so that he and Mama and any interested employees could attend. Coach and a lot of the team came, too. We were shocked when several of the Harrises walked in to pay their respects. Uncle Stuart must have gotten their attention. Dr. Byrd and her husband drove down. He and Mama had a fine time getting reacquainted. Pooch, Tol, Lady, and Buddy wore vests that Pauline had sewn. She had sewn letters spelling H-E-R-O on the back of Pooch's vest. Tol's and Lady's vests said G-O-O-D G-I-R-L. Buddy's said G-O-O-D B-O-Y. Zeus was not at all interested in attending and so did not receive a vest.

Winnie led the service, her first. She took her text from several places in the Bible—mainly Hebrews 13:2—"Be not forgetful to entertain strangers: for thereby some have entertained angels unawares." Vera sang songs that Bertie requested: "Angels We Have Heard on High," "Hark the Herald Angels Sing," and "Bicycle Built for Two" except instead of "Daisy, Daisy," Vera sang "Bertie, Bertie." Best we could figure Tom must have sung it to her. Bertie sat on the front row between Merril and Lee Harris. They held her hands. It was the first funeral all summer where she didn't act up.

All in all, it was a crying good funeral. We stood around in the churchyard and visited before several of us headed back to the big house for funeral food and goodbyes. The Altheans, except for Winnie, had packed their things and were going to strike out for home after eating. Merril had gotten her flight changed to 4:00 that afternoon. Dr. Byrd and her husband would drop her off at the airport on their way home. It was good that Merril had to catch a plane or nobody might have ever left.

Me-Mama asked the Altheans what they'd be working on for their senior theses. Dr. Byrd was interested in their responses because she had a feeling that she'd be involved. Winnie was planning on researching spiritualism and religion in the American South. Merril was considering an oral history of the Lily Dale community. Vera was intrigued by the prospects of turning Tom's story into a dramatic presentation for stage and screen. True to form, Sister figured something would come to her. Dr. Byrd shook her head, smiled, and said, "You may find yourself graduating in spite of yourself." Susie B. and Lee

Harris were glad that they were only going to be juniors and could avoid the subject.

This conversation went on for a while before Daddy, who fretted about missing a plane more than about anything, finally jumped in and said, "Merril, y'all need to get on your way in case you have a flat tire."

"Or three," Sister and Mama piped in unison.

"Yes sir. I know." Merril went around, hugged us all, and told us how much we meant to her. She whispered to me that she was expecting to read all about our glorious victory against Hannibal.

Finally, Peter handed her Tom's box. She held it close as she walked out the front door and down the steps. Peter followed with her suitcase. Me-Mama hollered after her, "You're always welcome." Granddaddy added, "You all are." Merril turned and waved before getting in the back seat. We watched from the porch as the Byrds' car made its way down the long driveway.

Tommy Reynolds going home was the last strange thing that happened that summer.

Acknowledgments

One of my goals has been to write something that people weren't assigned to read for a class report on conversational analysis or another topic academe. So many people have helped me try to achieve this goal that thanking them might take longer than writing the book itself. So, I'd like to take this opportunity to say 'preciate you to several folks who supported me along the way. (Please forgive me if I forget to call your name. Absentminded is right there in the description of a professor.)

Speedy and I hereby award keys to the City of Rowja to:

My remarkable, fun-loving parents and grandparents who inspired many of the episodes in this book—mom and dad, Nell and Bruce Brown and grandparents Happy and Ruby Brown. Even though you've gone on ahead of me, I still hear and often, or at least occasionally, follow your advice and counsel.

My ever so talented (almost) life-long mischief maker, my sister, Bonnie Jean Brown with whom I shared a bedroom, my rejected toys from the store, and my heart.

Various aunts, uncles, and cousins—especially Aunt Irene Christian, Aunt Helen Hooker, Aunt Julia Baldwin, and Aunt Chrissie Parker—for all the stories they told and provided.

Carol Clifford Turner and Amy Lynn Robertson, my friends for as long as I can remember having friends.

The fabulous Jay Lamar who took my offer to help clean out the attic and shifted it to an application to become the Breeden Scholar. You read Chapter One (written twenty+ years ago) and said "you must finish this" and then made it possible to do so.

Maiben Beard, Nancy Griggs, and the ghosts of Pebble Hill who kept me company.

Chief editor and reader extraordinaire, Marian Carcache, to whom I solemnly promise that pets will always be safe and happy in Rowja.

Rheta Grimsley Johnson and Karen Spears Zacharias for the kind words that left me speechless.

Portia Gaines who helped me discover how to write and who continues to read my work, including the very first draft of this book.

Hollie Lavenstein and Leah Ades Cooper who read drafts and provided great encouragement.

The amazing Jessie King for our Pho Lee meetings and assorted collaborations. You and the fine folk at createTWO—Kevin Smith, Katy Doss, Lillian Parker, Lindsey Baker, and Charissa Jones—have gone above and beyond anything I could hope for in Team Rowja.

Margaret Fitch-Hauser and Jennifer Adams from the School of Communication and Journalism and Anna Gramberg from the College of Liberal Arts at Auburn University for their support of my creative activities.

Tina Tatum, Laura Breitenbeck and all the other fine folks at Solomon and George Publishers who have made the publishing process as painless as possible.

Buddy (#8), Lady, Zane, Addy, Tater, and Junebug.

My partner in life's adventures, Beth Yarbrough. You have my gratitude forever and ever.

GO DOBBERS. BEAT HANNIBAL.

About the Author

Mary Helen Brown was born and raised in Center, Texas, where her parents Bruce and Nell Brown owned and operated Brown Drug Company. She and her sister, Bonnie, spent many hours on the family farm where Bonnie still resides. Mary Helen graduated from—take a breath—Center High School, Lon Morris College, Centenary College, the University of Kentucky, and The University of Texas. She served for more than thirty years as an associate professor of communication at Auburn University. During that time, she received several teaching awards.

Mary Helen lives in Auburn, Alabama and enjoys watching the Tigers play (especially baseball), traveling, and allowing her pets, Junebug and Tater, to interfere with any attempt to get something productive accomplished.

Headed for Home is Mary Helen's first novel, but don't assume you have heard the last from Rowja, Texas.

Questions for Book Groups

1. If you were casting a movie of this book, would you cast Speedy as a boy or a girl? How do you think your reading of the book would change if your perception of Speedy changed?

2. How would you categorize this book—coming of age, mystery, ghost story, humor, a combination of some or all, or something else entirely? What factors go into your decision?

3. What lessons can this book teach us about tolerance for all sorts of people?

4. Whom do you believe to be the true hero or heroes of this story—Speedy, one of the Altheans, Bertie, Peter, Doc, Pooch, or someone else?

5. What should Mr. Julian include in his historical context for the old high school yearbook advertisement for the KKK before he places it in the Bluebonnet?

6. Did Papa and Poodle make the right decision to bury Tom in secret? What else might or should they have done?

7. When the author has been asked what the book is about, she generally says, "there may be a ghost." Do you believe in ghosts? How might a belief in ghosts account for occurrences that may be difficult to explain otherwise?

8. "Home" in the book's title could refer to a number of places—home plate, the old homeplace (Aunt Catherine's farm), or to Tom's journey. Why is the concept of home so important to this story?

To Hannibal
BOO!
HISS!

To C

Woodrock
Methodist

Woodrock

OLD
GIN

tWoodrock
Baptist

Peter ·
Paul he's
H

Mimi's
house

BigHo

ly cemetery

Doc'

Taterhead
Creek

Our H

Head out
this way
and change
roads
to get to
Dallas

Rowj

FM 44 76

To
Nacogdoches

To Houston
(eventually)
GO ASTROS!

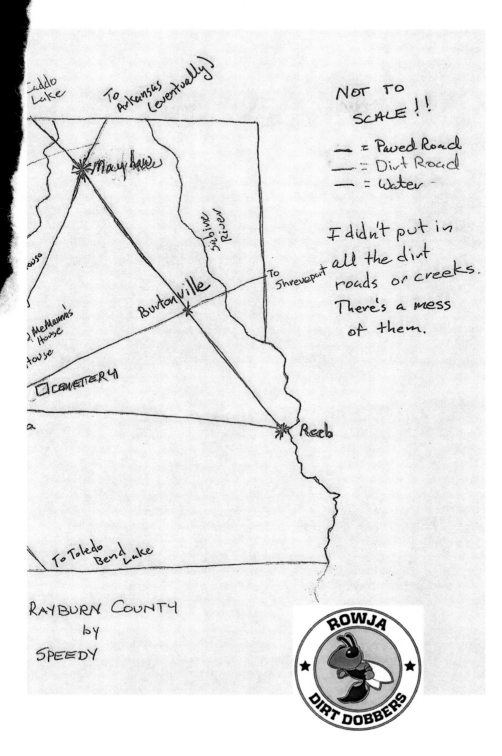

Caddo Lake

To Arkansas (eventually)

NOT TO SCALE !!

—— = Paved Road
—— = Dirt Road
—— = Water

I didn't put in all the dirt roads or creeks. There's a mess of them.

Mayhaw

Sabine River

To Shreveport

...ouse

...d McMann's House

...ouse

Burtonville

☐ CEMETERY

...a

Reeb

To Toledo Bend Lake

RAYBURN COUNTY
by
SPEEDY

ROWJA
DIRT DOBBERS